THIS BOOK IS DEDICATED WITH UTMOST RESPECT AND ADMIRATION TO THE PHILOSOPHY AND WRITINGS OF DR. HUNTER S. THOMPSON, AS WELL AS TO THE MAN HIMSELF. OUR STORIES STAND AS TRIBUTES TO HIS MEMORY.

JOHN BRUNI
KENT HILL
KEVIN CANDELA

COVER ART BY ANTHONY ELDRIDGE

(COVER ARTIST ANTHONY ELDRIDGE LIVES IN UT. WHEN ASKED ABOUT THE PAINTING HE SIMPLY SAID, "WE WERE 20 MINUTES OUTSIDE OF RACHEL, NV WHEN THE TRACTOR BEAM TOOK HOLD..." PHILOSOPHY: "I LIKE TO KEEP MYSTERY ALIVE AND A SENSE OF HUMOR EVIDENT.")

KHP
Kent Hill Publishing

CONTENTS

Brian — When the going gets hellish, the weird go monstering!

FEAR AND LOATHING IN HELL

John Bruni

1

An impostor. I am Ahab. Smoking weed in Hell. There's always time for Chivas. The First Circle. Fuck the doomed. Bat country. Four more years? The blood of Nixon.

"Jesus Christ, man! Get up! It's about time! Where were you?"

I jerk upright, and in this moment I know with absolute certainty that I'd gotten drunk while driving and had passed out. Someone had screamed at me to wake up. That's what happened. You bet. But then I look around and see no car. Not much of anything, really. Just me and *sweet Jesus*! My attorney! Last I heard, he'd disappeared. I imagine that he'd been murdered by savage drug kingpins.

7

He has to be an impostor. I grab for the can of Mace I keep on hand at all times, but my hand scrabbles at nothing but my belt. Very well. I have to handle this with my bare hands. I am Ahab.

I lunge for his throat, but the impostor moves too fast for me. He twists one of my arms up behind me and starts barking like a mad dog. I try to twist out of his grip, but the bastard has me. For good or ill.

"Stop!" the impostor shouts. "Calm down! I have some weed that'll take the edge off. Just stop, or I'll break your goddam arm!"

Weed? Well, that's a different story. Maybe this impostor isn't all that bad. My heart screams in my chest, and I need to level out. I stop moving. He lets me go and steps back, just in case I make any sudden moves. I can't blame him. I feel savage, and I need to thrash someone to get the beast out of my system.

He offers me a joint and his lighter, but he keeps his distance. I probably can't nail him, anyway. While I can be sudden, I don't have quite the reach as my attorney. I light up and let soothing smoke fill my insides. I take a few tokes, and before long I feel like a balloon.

"Jesus, man," my attorney says. "You had this look about you. I was afraid I'd have to put you down. Horrible. *Horrible.*"

"You're dead. I think. So you can't really be here. You also look the same as you did when we went to Vegas to find the American dream. Who are you, really?"

"I'm your attorney. And yeah, I'm dead. So are you."

I think. Therefore I am. Descartes said that, and I feel it applies to my situation. Come to think of it, I started this story in an odd place. I need action, but I never start in the middle of something, do I? But it is the first thing I can remember. I don't have time to settle into this article, like I usually do. What was I doing before this? Where was I? It feels like I'd been blackout drunk last night but without the hangover. I try to piece it together, but I come up with nothing.

"You killed yourself," my attorney says. "Now you're in Hell."

Bullshit. No, wait. I always figured I'd take the Hemingway if life got too rough. Had I gone out the way I wanted to? Driving a whale of a Cadillac at top speed off a cliff? I seem to remember a gun, but it's not very clear. Maybe a drunk memory.

"What's the booze situation?" I ask. "I think I need some Chivas to crack this nut."

"There's no time for that! We've got to hurry! This is a bad scene, man, and we have to stop it. You have no idea how long I've been waiting for you."

"Since the 'Seventies?"

"No, you fool! Time works differently down here! It's been waaaaaaay longer than that."

I snarl at him, my hand reaching for the .44 magnum I usually wear at home. Then I remember I'm not at home, but I still feel the need to shoot this bastard. "I knew you were an impostor! There's always time for Chivas! My attorney was a wise man, and he knew this fact."

He stops, his mouth hanging open like a hairy urinal, thinking. After a silent moment, he straightens up, smiling. "By God, you're right. I've been in this wasteland for too long. It has an effect on a man. Turns him into an unthinking beast. Let's go. There's a bar in the First Circle."

"Now you're making sense." I follow him to a nearby gate, and this thing looks like a medieval holdover from the Dark Ages. Rusty, covered in semen-like cobwebs with skeletal bodies hanging from it. Oddly, I think some of those skeletons are still alive, even though I don't see any of their plumbing. They groan, and the susurrus eases over me like a balm. Still, my danger sense goes off.

"I think we should be armed," I tell my attorney.

"That's a good idea." He stops, and from inside his suit he pulls out the biggest handgun I have ever seen. It looks like a .44 magnum, but double in size. Yet it felt as light as the air in my hand.

"What the hell is this thing?"

"It's a demon stopper," my attorney says. "Be careful with that thing. It's loaded."

He gives me a holster, and I put it on. I glance up and see a flock of bats flapping by. Bat country. Jesus, does my attorney know this? I turn to tell him this, but he looks directly into my eyes. He knows.

"It's all bat country down here," he says darkly.

We approach the gate, and I can't help but think of Dante's *Inferno*. "Abandon all hope, ye who enter here." Right. Comfort hangs just below my left arm, and it awaits us in a bar in the First Circle. Limbo, from what I remember. That sounds safe. I don't think we'd need guns just yet, but I always prepared for the worst regardless of expectation.

The gate screams as my attorney opens it up. We step through, and the air changes instantly. I reach for my cigarettes, but I don't have them. My adrenaline kicks up, and my heart races laps in my chest. My attorney sees this and offers me a pack, complete with a cigarette holder.

I feel almost human now. Beasts don't smoke with cigarette holders, you know. We move through the noxious fumes on our way to the little village we see on the horizon. Screams ring out in the distance, and I know we are right at home. We are ten feet high and bulletproof. Yes. If anyone fucks with us, we will beat them like gongs. Gods among men, we stride into town ready to stomp the terra and declare our dominion over it.

As we get closer to the screams, I can see where they're coming from. The road to town is lined with figures crucified to swastikas, all screaming their heads off, all dressed in what used to be fine suits.

"I thought this was Limbo," I say.

"Never mind that Dante gibberish," my attorney says.

"The First Circle is made up of hippies who grew up to vote Republican."

I stare at these screaming, writhing shapes and tried to imagine them with long hair or wearing bellbottoms. No. Their dapper shapes conceal any kind of soul they might have once had. Fuck them.

I feel a shock go down my spine. A memory, unbidden, suddenly whisks to the surface of my mind. "Fuck the doomed." Nixon said that, and now I feel a chill at the very thought that I might be saying the same thing. My attorney was right; this place tends to make a beast of men.

The village is empty, and I think it's because the occupants are all nailed up by their wrists. The Fear crawls up my spine with a knife in its teeth. I have to get out of here. It's too much for me. I draw my gun without even realizing it.

The tavern looks like any hole-in-the-wall neighborhood bar. Why is there a bar in an abandoned town? I consider asking my attorney, but I know I will get no answer that will make sense. Fine. I can deal with this. The tavern almost makes me feel at home. I relax a bit, but I don't holster my gun. I have a sense for these things. Bad craziness can spring on a man at any moment, and I have to be ready to wrestle this fucker to the ground and bite its nuts off.

The bartender is a middle-aged, balding man with a gut and a pin on his shirt declaring his pride in voting for Bush. I think he means Bush I. I resist the urge to pistol whip the swine.

"Relax, man," my attorney says. "You won't need that in here." Pointing at my gun.

I put it back under my arm and take a stool next to my attorney. I fold my arms on the bar so that my gun hand will be ready for any action.

"What can I get you boys?" the bartender asks.

"My client will have a triple Chivas, light on the

rocks," my attorney says. "I'll take a Motherfucker."

"Jesus!" I say. "What's a Motherfucker?"

"The only thing worth drinking down here. It's a mixture of well whiskey, tequila, a pinch of cocaine and a thimbleful of rat poison."

Jesus! My attorney's gone. He's lost the goddam plot, and it's up to me to handle things from here. "Maybe you should let me do the talking."

"I've got this, man. Relax."

The bartender comes back with our drinks, and my attorney reaches in his pocket, scrambling around for a moment. Then he places what looks like two teeth on the counter. They are chipped and have blood on them.

"Keep the change," he says.

My attorney must have noticed my confusion. He says, "Down here teeth are currency. Don't ask me why. Not much makes sense in this fucking wasteland. But I love getting 'em. There's something satisfying about punching a man in the face hard enough to crack his teeth out." He laughs and downs half of his drink.

Death had somehow made my attorney more savage than he'd ever been in life. I have to keep an eye on him. Never let him stand behind me. Don't let him have any sharp objects. Warily, I take a sip from my drink. The booze hits me instantly, and it rides the wave the weed has already built up inside my head. Perfect.

"Okay," my attorney says. "To business. Can you hear me?"

"Yes." I wonder why he suddenly asked me that. No music or noise would have overridden his volume. Is the rat poison going to work? My hand creeps closer to my gun.

"I've got some bad news for you, man. Real bad. I'm not going to sugarcoat it, so I'm just going to lay it on you. Nixon's here, and he's been elected Satan. Can you grasp that?"

I snarl and beat my fist on the bar. "That pigfucker! I

knew it!"

"Right, man. That's what I said. I've been waiting for you ever since that cocksucker arrived. I can't do this alone. I need your help."

Yes. Right. The worm has turned. I've always wanted to horsewhip that swine. Now is finally my chance. "Count me in."

My attorney pumps his fist at the air. "Yes! I knew you'd be in! It's great to ride with you again, man."

"But we'll need some supplies."

"Bartender! Get over here! We need things."

My attorney drops a fistful of teeth on the bar as I rattle off my list: a brick of weed, a pill bottle full of mescaline, as much blotter acid as my attorney can carry, a salt-shaker full of cocaine, a quart of Wild Turkey 101, a gallon jug of Motherfucker, a hypodermic loaded with Dilaudid, about fifty Vicodins for the pain, ether, some crank and two dozen amyls. I think maybe we should get a case of Flying Dog, but I don't know how we'd carry it into the depths of Hell.

The bartender loads it up into a briefcase, but not before I can grab the salt shaker and snort a rail the size of my finger. I set one up for my attorney, and he dives into it as he negotiates with the bartender. His whitened nostrils flare like a bull's as he works out a fair price. He only has to draw his Gerber Mini-Magnum once, and he doesn't even have to hold it to the bartender's throat. With pure menace, we manage to get out of the place without spending too many teeth. We also get a case of shit beer on the house. Not bad for a shithole in Hell. The crowning achievement, though, is the cherry red Chevy. It's vintage and reminds me of the shark from our Las Vegas assignment.

On the street, my attorney puts the knife away. "Jesus Christ. You have no idea how close I came to cutting his goddam teeth out. He's lucky I know the law. You ever see a blade cut into some poor bastard's gums?" He shudders as if horrified by himself. True enough. Hell is not for the weak of mind.

"You ready for this, man?"

"Wait." I root around in the case until I come up with the whiskey. I pop the cork and drink from the bottle. Its rejuvenating warmth spreads through me, taking the edge of the coke a bit. I level out, and I feel like I'm exactly where I'm supposed to be.

"Let's get this fucker and put him in the ground."

My attorney smiles at me. "I knew I liked you, man. Gimme the bottle."

He takes a healthy swig and hands it back. Whiskey glistens on his teeth, and he looks like a cannibal for a moment. My attorney is a scary beast, but he is my beast. Together we start on our path to the center of Hell, eager for the taste of Nixon's blood.

2

Mescaline in Hell. Checkers. And that's the way it is. Kuh meh. Raining blood. Worse than Nixon?

The mescaline kicks in as we drive through the heart of the third circle of Hell. Everything down here has a reddish tint to it, but now it crackled off the surface of reality. Sweat oozes out of every pore, and I try cranking the AC on the Chevy. Nothing happens.

"You fool," my attorney says. "No one's air conditioning works in Hell." His own face is covered in a shiny sheen, and I can barely see his facial features through it. I squint against the vibrant colors coming off of him and his Acapulco shirt. I'm wearing one, too, but I dare not look down at myself. The Fear slowly creeps over me, and I force my attention up. Bad move. The bats seem bigger than they've ever been, and now there were manta rays up there, bodies ululating like rippling laundry on a clothesline. Sweet Jesus! Look at the size of them! I don't know how much longer I can bear this.

My attorney thumbs the AC lever down, and even though I know it doesn't work, I somehow feel even hotter than before. Sheets of flame light up the horizon, and I can feel their goddam shadows on my face. I wipe the dampness from my forehead, but it does no good.

"Keep cool, man," my attorney says. "It's not that bad. Yet."

"Yet?! What do you mean by that, you savage?!"

My attorney draws his Gerber on me, and he holds it to my throat. He never removes his eyes from the road. "Don't get ugly, man. Just stay cool."

I remain silent, even though a crowd of words gets clogged in my throat. The best way to deal with a brute is to be quiet. Don't make any sudden movements. Let him think he's in control, and that he doesn't want to hurt you. I wait, and the blade comes away from me. My attorney sheathes it.

"Cool," he says. He runs his hand through his wild hair. "Get some of the acid. I think that's what I need to make this perfect."

How cam he be thinking of acid at a time like this? His time down here has truly driven him mad. This does not stop me from reaching into the backseat for our case of drugs. He sticks out his tongue, and I place a tiny square on it. For a moment I consider his lunatic courage, and I can't let him do this without me. I pop a square into my own mouth and feel it dissolve.

Yes. For good or ill, we are doing this. We will kill like champions.

The car slows, and at first I wonder if the acid hit my attorney a little too badly. He pulls over to the curb and turns off the ignition. Panting, he looks up to the building we're next to.

"What is this?" I ask. "I thought you were made of sterner stuff than this acid."

"No. We need to make a stop here. There's something

inside that we need in order to cripple Nixon. Watch my back, man."

He gets out of the car, and I follow him up to the front door. He draws his Gerber, so I draw my magnum. Things start dancing at the corners of my eyes, but I don't have time to deal with the acid now. My adrenaline rushes, and I am ready for battle.

He enters, and he holds a finger to his mouth. "This circle is for journalists who lied about important things. Every one of these buildings is stuffed with them, all the way back to Herodotus. They spend the rest of eternity with their feet in snarling dogs' mouths."

"That's heavy." I cast my mind back, trying to think of some time that I lied about something important. Nothing comes to mind, but who can say for sure about these things?

"Don't worry. If you were one of these animals, you would have been sent to this circle instead of the gates. You'd have your feet in a Doberman's jaws. Or worse."

I can't bear the thought. I grip my gun tighter, and he leads me up the stairwell. I can see his heartbeat through his back. I can probably see mine, too, but I won't look down. Maybe we should have forgotten this rotten mess and gotten twisted with ether instead.

"What do we need here?" I ask.

My attorney chuckles deep in the back of his throat. "You'll see. I think you'll like this, man."

We stop at the sixth floor, and we go down the corridor until we find room sixty-six. One of the sixes is upside down on its nail, but we know it for what it is. Is this some kind of joke my attorney has cooked up? Why? I thought he was in a hurry to get to Nixon, right?

My attorney rears back with his foot and clobbers the door right next to the doorknob, just like a cop. The door caves in, sent asunder in jagged pieces. Even the hinges are snapped. He roars, knife at the ready, and charges into the room.

In the very center is a bound and gagged man. Wait, that's not right. The gag is actually stapled to his face, and his hands are nailed to the chair arms. His legs are bound with razor wire except for his bare feet. Those are gripped in the firm jaws of a cocker spaniel.

In a moment of absolute horror, I recognize the man as Walter Cronkite. I didn't even know he'd died. I would have heard about something like this. I can't think of a reporter more trusted by America, and he's in this ugly place? He covered the Nuremburg trials, for Christ's sake. He gave us the news about JFK's vicious murder under the unforgiving Texas sun. How many years had he reported? Fifty? More? Could a man in the midst of that many American news stories really be honest? How many of us can make a claim like that?

"Gotcha, you bastard!" My attorney grabs the dog around its throat and yanks as hard as he can. The dog's teeth are set in deep, and Walter Cronkite screams through his bloody gag. It's a spine tingling sound, like when a squirrel yelps in pain. I feel tempted to end Wally's agony with one well-placed .44.

My attorney jabs the dog in the throat with the knife hilt, and it only growls. Normally the beating of a helpless animal makes me queasy, but somehow I get the feeling that this dog is tougher than it looks. I back away and let my attorney go to work, wrestling the cocker spaniel like some kind of grim Hulk Hogan show. Then he starts aiming the blade for the eye.

"Jesus man," I say. "It's just a dog."

"We need this dog," he says. Teeth gritted like a warrior-to-be going through his coming-of-age trial. A Lakota boy doing the Sun Dance. "But we don't need it in one piece."

I grimace, but I don't look away as my attorney lightly taps the tip of his Gerber on the surface of the dog's eye. It shrieks, and finally its teeth are gone from Walter Cronkite's feet. My attorney drags the dog backwards and clamps his hands around its muzzle. It tries to fight back and open up, and it almost succeeds.

"Quick, man!" he says. "I need to bind this bitch's mouth shut! Get that razor wire!"

I don't know if I want to take part of his savage paean to animal cruelty. But then my attorney glares at me with his drug-fueled, swirling eyes. I go to Walter Cronkite's legs, and I gingerly untie the wire, mindful of the razors.

"Faster, man!"

"I'm going as fast as I can, you pigfucker!" I finally get the wire off of him, and I help my attorney wrap it around the dog's muzzle. He ties a rough knot around the dog's mouth and then uses the rest of the wire to bind its legs together. It looks like a hogtied steer.

"Gotcha, you bitch." My attorney stands and admires his work. I expect him to start branding the poor animal next, but he only rests back with his arms akimbo.

"That was needlessly violent," I say. "Are we already at that stage in this mad journey?"

"Don't you get it, man? That's not any dog."

I look at the whimpering beast, and it does seem kind of familiar.

My attorney sighs. "Try this on for size: 'One other thing I probably should tell you because if we don't they'll probably be saying this about me, too. We did get something—a gift—after the election. A man down in Texas heard Pat on the radio mention the fact that our two youngsters would like to have—'"

"A DOG!" I suddenly scream. "Jesus Christ! This is Checkers!"

"Nixon loves this dog more than life itself. He has no idea it's down here. I intend to use Checkers against him. I'm not fucking around here, man. I want him to be utterly destroyed."

"That dog never did anything to us," I say.

My attorney snarls, and he presses the hilt of the knife to his forehead, eyes closed, nostrils flaring like a bull's.

"You don't get it, man. We need to be killers. Nixon has to respect our violence. We can't get that unless we prove to him we're willing to do anything."

"Anything? Hell, is Pat Nixon down here? Maybe we can throw a good raping down on her. That would freak Nixon out, right? How *far* are we going with this?"

"That's not the point, man. You can violate her if that's your trip, but I don't think that will hurt him. No, hurting this dog in front of him will really get to him. He'll lose it, and he'll be right where we need him."

I hadn't meant to get him going on a rape trip. I'd said that only to show how crazy he was acting. Hell has driven him so far beyond humanity that he isn't in a rational mind frame. I have to calm him down.

"Listen. We'll bring the dog with us, sure. Let's just go down and get into some weed. That'll get us thinking a bit more clearly."

His eyes open, and he points the knife in my direction. His crazy eyes are fixed on mine. "I'm thinking more clearly than I've ever thought before."

Walter Cronkite whimpers. He tries to say something through his gag. I think it's, "Mercy." I can't be sure though. He turns his watery, red eyes on me. "Kuh meh. Peese."

It's the only reasonable thing to do. I put the barrel against his forehead, and his eyes squeeze shut.

"It's no use, man," my attorney says. "If you shoot him like that, he'll spend the rest of eternity like that, being aware of his mutilated head the whole time. Can you grasp that? Imagine having your head blown all over the place and being stuck in that moment forever?"

Jesus. This grim place couldn't get worse. I lower the weapon. "Sorry Wally. It would only make life down here worse. Cheer up, though. At least your legs are free, and you don't have a dog on your feet."

The door opens, and another dog—this one a bulldog —enters. It clamps its slobbery jowls down on Walter

Cronkite's lacerated feet, and he screams through his gag. "Whoops," I say. "I guess that's the way it is. Well, we'll leave now. Good luck with that, Wally. Don't take any guff from the swine."

I can't look at him anymore as I head for the exit. I thunder down the stairs, and I can hear my attorney lumbering behind me. When we get back to the street, I see that he brought Checkers with him. He throws the dog into the backseat and gets behind the wheel himself. He looks at me.

"Daylight's wasting, man. Let's go."

I look up to the sky. There is no daylight. Either that or the mescaline is through with me. I dive into the passenger seat, but not before I roll a couple of joints. I hand one of them to my attorney, and he holds it in his thick, rubbery lips, jutting it out to me. I light it, and he puffs.

"That hit the spot, man. You were right. Weed is perfect for this moment."

I light my own joint, but it's not enough to perish the sense of impending doom that weighs heavily on my heart. This journey is already taking a dark turn. I hope we can get through this without turning into something worse than Nixon.

My face is wet, and when I touch it, I see blood on my hands. It is suddenly all around me. It is pouring from the sky in a light drizzle. If this isn't an omen of the bad craziness to come, I don't know what is.

My attorney is unfazed by this sudden development, but I am entranced by his shirt. The patterns are moving around his body, and I suddenly remember the acid. Jesus! What was I thinking? Acid is the wrong drug for a scumhole like this. I can only hope that the weed evens out my trip and makes it tolerable.

My attorney hits the accelerator, and we jerk toward the next circle of Hell.

20

3

There can be no evidence. The Extractor. Angels in Hell. Sweet revenge. The return of Junkie George. Buy land.

The acid is kind to me, and it doesn't give me more than a mild mushroom-type trip. The land ululates gently, hypnotically, and my mind wanders. The rest of this circle passes by without any trouble, and this journey seems almost human for at least a little while.

And then I realize the horrible mistake I've made. "We've got to turn back!" I scream.

My attorney ignores me. He is muttering under his breath, and while I can see the soundwaves this causes, I can't actually hear the bastard. Is he a cop? Do I have The Fear? Yes. No. I'm not sure. This must stop.

"Turn back, you swine! Or I'll put the goddam leeches on you!"

He opens his shirt a little, just enough so I can see the butt of his .357 snub nose revolver. "There are no laws down here, man. I can kill you, and no one will give a fuck."

I think I can take him. The barrel of my .44 is longer than his, and it might snag, but remember: I'm sudden. Wait, this is wrong. We can't be at each other's throats, not at this crucial moment in our mission. This place. It can turn an elephant into a scheming hyena. I must try a diplomatic tone.

"You don't understand. I'm a journalist. I should be taking down all of the details of what we're doing. I'm going to at least need a reel-to-reel tape recorder to dictate into."

"No. There can be no evidence." He turns his eyes on me, and they are yellow and slitted, like a lizard's. The acid is not done with me yet. This might get ugly.

"This is about the truth!" I hear my mouth roaring. I have to reel myself in before things get out of control, but

I can't. The acid surges in my brain.

He grimaces, and his teeth revolve around in his mouth like a reverse chainsaw, sparking against each other. "As your attorney, I advise you to forget recording this."

"Never mind that gibberish! There's no law down here. You said so!"

Sweat runs down his large, basketball head, and for a moment, I think this is it. He's going to reach for the gun. Instead, he laughs. "You're right. I did say that. We'll get the recorder, but I'm almost out of teeth."

"How do we get those down here?" I ask.

"Don't worry about that, man. We'll get some more." There is something I don't like about the gleam in his eye. It reminds me of "The Tell-Tale Heart." I can suddenly hear his pulse. I can even see it running through the veins on his hands, clenched tightly around the steering wheel.

We saw the road marker for the next circle. To take his mind off such ominous thoughts, I decide to change the subject. "So. What's this circle dedicated to?"

My attorney chuckles. "I think you'll like this one. This is where all bikers go when they die. I'm sure there are a lot of Hell's Angels down here, and I know how you feel about them."

Yes. Indeed. Generally I like them, at least the ones who were cool with me. There is a handful of them I wouldn't mind meeting down in this lawless place with two pistols clutched in my hands. A thought occurs to me.

"I think we should get the teeth we need from these pigfuckers."

My attorney smiles. "That's what I was thinking. But cracking teeth out of people with our bare hands is going to tear up our knuckles. We'll need gloves."

"Never. Not when I have the butt of my trusty .44 magnum."

"That's a good idea, man. Here, there's a blackjack

in the backseat. Grab that, would you? And maybe a couple of beers."

I get the beers first. We must have priorities. Then, after scrabbling around blindly with one hand I find the blackjack on the floor. I heft the bastard, and I almost feel sorry for anyone who would fall under it. I give my knee a light tap, and a quick but sharp pain lights up. I give it a closer examination and I see a lot of scuffing and marks along with some dried blood.

"I call it the Extractor," my attorney says darkly.

I reverently place it on the seat next to me, and my hand hangs over it, eager for its first use. I down the warm beer in one gulp and toss it over the edge. I can hear it clunk off the road several times before it comes to rest in a ditch with others like it. Many drinkers have made this trek, and their leavings line the way. It reminds me of the old days before people started giving a shit about the environment. It feels good to revert to the old ways. In the distance I see smokestacks, all of them proudly billowing poisonous gases. The red smog. That must be where the blood rain comes from.

"I'm getting too sentimental," I say. "We're going to need to pick up the pace. Pull over. I want to get into the trunk and get some amyls."

"You're the doctor," my attorney says.

As soon as the car comes to a stop, I hop out and get into the trunk. The kit is already open, and my fingers run greedily over our drug collection. I stuff my pockets with amyls, and after a moment's thought I grab the baggie of crank and the salt shaker of coke, and I pocket them as well. If we run into the Angels, we'll need it.

I hear the dog whining in the backseat, and I think what the hell? Why not make Checkers feel a bit more comfortable. I grab a Vicodin and crush it up with the butt of my gun. Then I drop the crumbs into a beer. Gingerly, I pull the dog's lips back and pour the entire beer through Checkers's teeth.

"What are you doing?" my attorney asks.

"Making Checkers feel better. He's cranky and must be calmed down."

"One beer's not going to do it. Make it two."

"No! I put a Vicodin in this."

"Oh. Yeah. That will do it."

The crumbs of the pill stick to the dog's teeth. I close its mouth and let saliva do its work. I take a quick nip or three of the Wild Turkey before I close the trunk and hop back in. I hand two of the amyls to my attorney, and he cracks them both, breathing them in at the same time.

He roars like a beast and starts beating his chest. "I AM KING MOTHERFUCKING KONG!"

"Yes! Right!" Keeping both eyes on my attorney, just to make sure he makes no sudden movements, I crack one of the amyls. It picks me up right away. I stiffen and tremble against its power. I can probably horsewhip someone with my dick . . . but that would be rude, even in this lawless and savage place.

"WE HUNT THE MOST DANGEROUS GAME! AND WE EAT WHAT WE KILL!"

"We do, indeed." Why argue with the man? At this point he will say a lot of odd things, and I will agree with each and every one of them, or we'll be at each other's throats again. I don't think I can take that again. Yet.

The rest of the acid works out of my system, and the stimulants start to take effect. To give them a helping hand, I crack the other amyl as my attorney starts singing something in a foreign language at the top of his lungs. I don't know what it is, but he seems to take a lot of pride in it despite slurring some of the words.

And then, finally, we hear a roar in the distance. It is loud enough to overtake my attorney's singing. We recognize the sound, and we glance at each other, grinning.

"We're coming up on a biker bar I know," he says.

"The Angels hang out there all the time. Maybe you'll see a few familiar faces."

"Indeed."

We crest a hill, and on the other side we see this rundown shit-pit surrounded by motorcycles and neon. The biggest neon tits I have ever seen reside over the door of this greasy establishment, and even from this distance, I can smell the BO of about twenty (20) Hells Angels. It stinks of whiskey and sex. I cradle the Extractor like a baby.

My attorney parks the car, and we get out. He starts toward the biker bar, but I grab his arm. He nearly freaks out. I can see him fighting the urge to lash out. He clenches his teeth and grinds them together. "Don't grab me like that."

"We're not ready for this madness. Here. Take some of these. On top of the amyls, it will turn us into gods." I give him two bennies, and he downs them with a can of beer. He groans like a dying beast.

"What have you done to me?" he whispers.

"Here. A spoonful of sugar helps the medicine go down." And I hand over the salt shaker.

"You're the doctor." He shoves the tip of the salt shaker into one of his cavernous nostrils and inhales deeply. He does the same with the other nostril, and he looks more alert than I've ever seen him.

I down my own pills, and when my attorney hands back the salt shaker, I have my dessert. I can see air molecules. I think I see the seams where the universe was stitched together, and maybe, just maybe, I can find the loose thread and pull the whole goddam thing apart. Yes.

No. I have a mission. Right. My attorney leads the way to the door and to the bouncer. Music blares out of the building from behind him. ZZ Top, I think.

"Members only," he says.

"This man is my client," my attorney says. "He is a close personal friend of Sonny Barger, and he rode with

the Angels many times. Are you prepared to go to court?"
The bouncer gives me a once over. "You don't look like an Angel to me."
"Right. Well, gang rape is low on my list of priorities."
A mean look crosses his face. He's about to say something, but my attorney viciously pistol-whips him across the nose. Blood explodes out of the bouncer's face, and he collapses to the ground, gagging and choking but unconscious.
"We're in a hurry," my attorney says. "After you, man."
He opens the door for me, and I enter with my .44 in one hand and the Extractor in the other. My blood is gold, and my voice is vengeance. But also I am a beast on two legs. A dangerous beast, and I can smell blood despite the stink of unwashed asshole in this twisted place.
Angels fill the building from wall to wall as do their women. They maybe had a full head of teeth between them all. I see a few familiar faces, some I'm even friendly with, some I know I will have to bludgeon because of rule ten. Or maybe it's eleven. I forget the details. If an Angel punches a non-Angel, the other Angels must also beat the mortal shit out of the non-Angel. I learned that first hand.
As I think this, I see the scumbag I'm looking for in particular. It's Junkie George. I remember it like it was yesterday. I saw him hitting his wife, and I told him, "Only a punk beats his wife." What followed was a flurry of punches and kicks. Junkie George's buddies beat seven shades of shit out of me. I've not taken a beating since then quite like it, and I never intend to ever again.
I see the others who stomped me hanging around Junkie George, and my blood is up. I do not think a warning is appropriate for this kind of thing, but I have drugs on my side. I pause for another quick snort from the salt shaker, and now I'm in the proper mindframe for

this kind of thing.

I sidle up on his blindside, and I roar so he can hear me over the roadhouse rock: "HEY JUNKIE GEORGE! TURN AROUND YOU FUCKING DINGBAT!"

He turns, a grin on his face, thinking he's about to see an old friend from long ago. I promptly bash that grin off his face with the Extractor. Teeth dribble down his shirt, and the look of shock on his face is so complete that I can only assume his brain hasn't registered the pain yet. I don't give him a chance. I swing at his temple, and his skull dents in on itself. He collapses. I don't know if he's dead. Can you even die in the afterlife? Then I think of Walter Cronkite's plea, and I smile.

One of Junkie George's friends makes a move on me, and I hold up the .44. "You want some of this, you scumsucker?! Huh? HUH?!"

The Angels crowd around us, champing at the bit, pulling out their own weapons. Chains and clubs and blades mostly, but the bartender draws down on us with a double barreled shotgun. My attorney calmly blows his brains out with his .357. "I got your back, man. Take these motherfuckers."

A chain lashes out at me, but these bastards are just like the other Angels: they don't know how to handle their high. They let it handle them. They don't realize who they're fucking with. I duck the chain, and I shoot the bastard in the throat.

They've started in on my attorney, too, but he can handle himself. We stand back to back in the crowd of animals, and we calmly do battle. We are professionals, after all. These things are just dumb brutes. They have the numbers, but we have the ability.

One of the swine gets a good shot in on my attorney. An overhead stab flashes behind me, and now he has a knife sticking out of his back high and to the right. It's not deep, but it remains in place even after my attorney dispatches the offender with a knife slash across his throat. I glance down and see that we are now wading in an ever expanding pool of blood.

He continues to fight even with the knife in his back. I admire him. No one else I'd rather be with in this battle to the death. I roar and beat someone's face off his skull.

Their women were interested in the fight at first, but now they're edging toward the backdoor. Good news. I don't advocate hurting women, but if one comes at me with a weapon and the intent of killing me, I have to do something.

Between the two of us, my attorney and I brutally kill about thirty of the Hell's Angels, and they're still coming at us. I feel like I'm in some kind of epic battle scene like the kind Homer wrote about. Men who fought for days on end before one of them finally succumbed to the other's violence or his own stamina. A chain wraps around my ankle, and someone tries to yank me off balance. I'm not an amateur. Once I noticed this, I stomp on the chain, and it goes slack.

My attorney and I are very careful with our weapons. I go to work with the Extractor when he fires his gun. Then he reloads, and I start using my gun. When I'm firing, he uses his blade, and when I reload, he goes back to his gun. We are two giant cogs in a killing machine, and we are very efficient.

"I'm almost out," my attorney says. "How are you doing?"

I fire my last bullet, nailing an Angel in the guts. "I'm dry."

There are still about ten of these bastards, and I don't know if we can take them without bullets. "The shotgun," he says. "Go for it. I'll cover you."

He fires three more times, and I leap into action. There is only one Angel between me and the bar, and I give him a healthy thump to the gonads. The air rushes out of him, and he clutches what must be two popped testes and a broken dick. He hits the floor with his face so hard I think he breaks his skull. Then I leap over the bar like a monkey, and I tear the shotgun from the bartender's cold dead hands. I hear my attorney's gun click on an empty chamber, and I rise like Satan himself, the shotgun double cocked.

"Get down!" I scream to my attorney. He drops and rolls toward the bar. When I deem he is out of range, I fire into the remaining seven Angels. Good luck to me: they are grouped conveniently together. Buckshot sizzles the air, and they are all peppered with it. Six of them get it so badly that they're torn to pieces. The seventh only gets a few of them in his arm.

Anyone else would have gone down. Not an Angel. He grits his teeth and rushes forward, his club in the air and ready for us.

My attorney strikes like a snake. The Gerber nails the Angel in the guts, and my attorney jerks up. The Angel's guts plop out of him, steaming like a pig's. He's alive, though, so I jump over the bar and bash his teeth out.

"Goddam. We got those fuckers," my attorney says.

"Indeed," I say. "Help me knock out their teeth."

Some of them are still alive when I use the Extractor on them, but by the time we have two giant sacks of teeth, there isn't a soul left in there but us. I also find a can of Mace, which I promptly strap to my belt. I also find a bullhorn, and that will undoubtedly come in handy.

My attorney goes behind the bar and takes down a bottle of mescal. He takes a long swig off of it and smiles, his scant facial hair glistening with alcohol. "We killed like champions, man. I've never felt so exhilarated."

"Think we got enough teeth to get us that recorder?" I ask.

"Shit. We have enough to buy all of Hell. As your attorney, I advise you to buy up all the land you can get.

It's always a valuable commodity."

"By God, you're right." I think that maybe after we take care of Nixon, perhaps we can set up our version of Woody Creek down here. My attorney would never go for it, though. He's too violent for such places.

4

The recorder. Pigs in Hell. Swine and blood. We've been here before. My attorney's wings. Running out of drugs. Who lives in Satan's asshole?

We buy the reel-to-reel recorder and a few spools from a pawn shop in the fourth circle from a man with a head shaped like a football and a severe case of asthma. He couldn't complete a sentence without running out of breath, and he panted like a sick dog, face red and uneven. I caught a bad vibe off of him, so we got out of there as quickly as we could.

Now we're driving over the hill and into the fifth circle. It looks like a vast desert, and the acid I dropped turns it into a wavering sea of nothingness. Cacti reach their prickled limbs out to me, and I warn my attorney about them. They're forming an arch over our car, and I think they're trying to shoot out their needles at me. I'm not a needle kind of guy, which is probably why I'm not going to get into the Dilaudid. I'll leave that heavy shit for my attorney. He still hasn't gotten his knife wound looked at. I think he'll need some painkillers. Shit, does he even *feel* pain? I don't know. He barely noticed it when I pulled it out of him in the biker bar parking lot.

"You're losing it," my attorney says. "Those fucking cactuses are all the way over there. They're nowhere near us."

"Cacti," I say.

"What the fuck is that?"

"It's the plural of 'cactus,' you fucking Samoan

savage!'"

He snarls, and I see murder in his eyes, which are painted on the outside of his sunglasses. "Stop that kind of talk, man. I'm not Samoan, and you know it. You white people are all alike."

He pulls over, and my danger sense tingles. I think he's finally ready to kill me. My hand wanders to the butt of my .44, but not in a way he'll notice. I'm glad that he had the spare ammo in his trunk. But that also means that he, too, has a loaded weapon. He's still riding high on crank and amyls. I must watch him carefully.

"Open the trunk," he says.

No. He's going to shove me in the back and drive the rest of the way with me in cramped darkness. That is not going to happen. Not while I have weapons. Not while I have Mace.

"I'm not locking you in the trunk," my attorney says.

Jesus! Can he read my mind? Or did I say that out loud?

"I just want you to get the ether."

"So the time has finally come, eh?"

"Not for me. For you. Besides, I'm driving."

I get out, but I keep a close eye on him as I go to the back and open the trunk. I don't look away from him. I find the bottle of ether by touch, and I whip out my handkerchief. I douse it with ether and suck a deep, rotten breath of it in.

I have just enough time to close the trunk and get back in before my limbs become rubbery. I sit down, and my body expands into a gooey puddle. What have I done to myself? This is irresponsible of me. I should be recording this, but I no longer have a body. I concentrate, trying to form a finger so I can press record. I remain stagnant.

"Press record," I try to say to my attorney. Something else comes out, though. Garbled gibberish. But that's fine. He can read my mind. I send these thoughts to him as hard as I can.

"Jesus, man," he says. "You're a mess." But he turns on the recorder.

I babble as best I can, and the car moves ever forward. How can I see without eyes? Or are my eyes just floating on the surface of my puddle body? I can still smell the dry desert around us, so I must have a nose. And I hear my attorney singing Jefferson Airplane, so I must have ears. Why can't I see them? I'm dripping all over the upholstery. I hope my attorney got insurance for this thing. I don't think the magazine will pay for any expense account that includes dripping my body all over the inside of a Chevy.

Am I on assignment? Who am I working for? Something about Nixon, but he died years ago. What the fuck? The ether renders me helpless, but the acid still burns its fever through the addled remnants of my brain. The cacti are growing up through the floor of the car, I think because my goo has eaten through to the desert. Or maybe one of them impregnated me. I don't remember any of this.

I start screaming. None of this makes sense. In this moment, I remember blowing my brains out. The pain of it sinks into what remains of my body, and I can think of nothing else. I died. Holy Jesus, I died! What am I doing here?

"Stop!" my attorney shouts. "The pigs, man."

Pigs in Hell? Ha! But then it makes sense. When the pigs die, they have to go somewhere. It's certainly not going to be the other place. My eyes are on fire, and I remember being tear gassed in Chicago in '68. Never again. No sir, they will never get Mrs. Thompson's boy again. But how can I hold a gun with a hand made of gloop?

My attorney pulls over the car, and a hulking beast of a man approaches the driver side door. He wears a CHiPs helmet over a hog's skull. He speaks without lips, and even though he has no eyes, I can see him glaring at me.

For some reason, I think he's trying to set me on fire with just a thought. Can I read his mind? I think so.

"Please excuse my client, officer," my attorney says. "This man is very sick, but I have his medicine. He's just having an episode."

The magic words. I can deal with the pig. I keep quiet, and I try to stop dripping. Keep it together. I've done this before. Dealing with cops is my specialty.

My attorney hands over a few teeth, and the pig nods. "On your way. And take care of that man. He looks like shit."

"Thank you, sir." My attorney starts driving again, slowly and in control. He stares into the rearview mirror, grimacing. "You nearly did us in, man. He was going to kill us."

I try to say something, but he ignores me. I ramble on into my recorder for a while, and I can feel my body coming back together. Before long I know where I am and what I'm doing. Right. I pressed stop and rewound the tape. I pressed play and listened to the nonsense I'd been spewing on my ether binge. None of it is cohesive. Near the end, when I started sobering up, I was able to form complete sentences. None of it made sense, but at least I can grasp it. This is the last thing I said on that tape:

"Someone tried to sneak up on me to prove their dominion, but I gutted them with a rock. Nothing stands between me and a good history lesson. Right. Blood and the Golden Rule has murdered the unbelievers. The streets run with swine and blood. And many rocks."

"Poetry, man," my attorney says. I can't argue with that. I press record again and put the machine in the backseat with the dog. The seat is wet, and I sniff my hand.

Piss.

I glance into the back and see that the dog has rolled around in its own piss and shit. When did this happen?

"We should have maybe gotten this thing a diaper," I say.

My attorney turns around, oblivious to the road in front of him, and looks into the backseat. "You bitch!" he screams. "I ought to rip your goddam head off and feed you to the coyotes!"

The car drifts, and I grab the wheel, pulling us back from the shoulder of the road. "You're driving angry. Maybe I should drive."

My attorney turns back to the front of the car, and it looks like he's ready to chew the steering wheel off. "I'm calm. Get me a fucking beer."

There's still a full bottle in the back, and it's not wet. It is warm, though, and my attorney pounds it down and throws the dead soldier behind him. "That hit the spot."

I'm still looking at the dog, and there's something familiar about him. In fact, this whole journey fills me with an atavistic sense. The desert around us moves like a conveyor belt past both sides of us, and for an odd moment, I feel like we're on some kind of soundstage in Hollywood.

"We've been here before," I say.

"No, man. You're just thinking of Las Vegas."

True. 1972 comes rushing back to me. Our search for the American Dream. We only ever found its corpse. God is dead. What of it? So is Nietzsche, and no one gives a fuck about him.

We drive for a while longer, and my attorney pulls over again. "This is no good. I'm crashing too hard, and for some reason, my goddam back is killing me."

"About here?" I ask. My finger comes down very close to the open knife wound.

He howls like a banshee. "Goddammit! That's the spot!"

"That explains everything. One of the Angels stabbed you there."

"What? When?"

"When we were in that bar, killing dozens of them."

"We *did* that?" A confused look comes over my attorney's face. His forehead is wrinkled like a worn shirt. "I thought that was a dream."

"Wait right here. I have just the thing for you. And move over. I'm driving for a while."

The car shakes from the massive weight of my attorney crawling over to the passenger side. I pop the trunk and locate the hypodermic needle full of Dilaudid. There is also a cable back here, so I use it to tie off his arm.

"Make a fist," I say. When he does, a clear blood vessel rises in the crook of his elbow. I slap it a few times.

"What are you doing?" he asks.

"I'm making you well. This should do the trick."

"Don't stab me! Give me the Vicodin! The Vicodin!"

"That's not going to cut it," I say. "Now stop moving. You don't want me to miss, do you?"

This calms the brute down, and I manage to nail the vein. As soon as I push the plunger down, I feel his body slacken. I don't want to give him the whole needle, but I think half of it is appropriate for this situation. His eyes close, and he has a beatific look on his face. He looks so calm that I consider shooting the rest of it, myself. But no. That's a kind of trip I don't want to get involved with this late in the game.

While my attorney is locked into an opiate stupor, I gently remove his .357 from its holster. There's no telling what level of depravity we'll sink to in Hell, but I feel better without him having a firearm.

I go back to the trunk. The drive will undoubtedly be long, so I need a stimulant, but I don't want to chew my own face off. I figure if I take a ton of crank, I can be alert and still keep calm if I drink some Wild Turkey while I drive. I down about five pills, and I bring the whiskey bottle to the driver's seat with me.

"Do I keep driving down this road? For how long?"

My attorney grimaces, and he doesn't want to talk. No, he wants to enjoy his high. He says, "Second star to the right and straight on till morning."

The last thing I expect from my attorney is a Peter Pan quote, but what the hell? We have only one direction right now. I can always wake him up if we later come to a crossroads or a town. I take a healthy belt of the Turkey and stomp on the accelerator. It occurs to me that there might be more Hell pigs out there, but we're in a wide open area. Nothing to hide behind. I feel confident in my ability to spot the fuckers before they can see us. My vision is better than 20/20, and my eyes refuse to close even in this godforsaken, dry desert.

Over the next two hours I manage to maintain the perfect buzz. Nothing can go wrong. We not only are going to win this thing, but we already *have* won it. This has happened many times before, and it will happen many times more, always with the same results. I will stomp Nixon's throat into paste, and then I'm going to put his head on the hood of this Chevy as an ornament. I know. I've done it before, and I'll do it again into eternity. A thousand million billion me's brutally murdering a thousand million billion Nixons, forever.

The whiskey bottle is empty, so I hurl it back behind me. I can't even hear it shatter on the road, the wind is whipping by so swiftly. The roar of the vehicle's engine makes for great white noise. My high is slowly coming down, though, and fatigue is setting in. Maybe I should stop and see what we have left in the drug kit.

My attorney stirs next to me. He groans, rubbing the open knife wound in his back. "Those goddam bastards took my wings," he says.

"What wings?" I ask.

"My angel's wings. I'm from Heaven, you know. But now I'm stuck in this place, and they ripped off my wings. I'm going to get them back. Mark my words."

"You never had wings, you dingbat! You were stabbed

in the back by a Hell's Angel! Pull yourself together!"

He grits his teeth. "It hurts too much. I need more of the Dilaudid."

Jesus. I'm turning him into a junky. He's fiending already. What have I done? When dealing with a junky in need, there is only one course of action. "I gave it all to you."

"Don't bullshit me, man. I know how much you gave me. You still have half of the needle. I need you to give it to me now." He holds out his arm, already making a fist.

"I did it," I say. "I injected myself with it after you passed out."

"Liar." He reaches for his gun, and I'm grateful for my forward thinking.

"It just smoothed me out. I have a high tolerance for opiates."

He grabs the back of my neck, and something cold presses against my throat. I see in the rearview mirror that it's a knife. I forgot about the Gerber. Jesus fuck! What is wrong with me? I'm getting forgetful in my old age.

"Pull over now," my attorney says. He glares at me like a bull looking at a matador's red cape, and his nostrils flare.

"You wouldn't dare slit my throat," I say. "I'll crash this goddam shark."

"Maybe I'll just cut a Z in your forehead." He shifts the blade until it's gently touching the space between my eyebrows. He lives, indeed. What would the Deputy do, then? Let the military take over and ban art? No, the scum murdered him. They won't get me. No.

Never argue with a drug. I pull over. "Take it easy. I'm just going to the trunk for your medicine."

He withdraws the Gerber, and I back out of the car, hands up in a surrendering gesture. I never take my eyes off him, not until I get to the trunk. I take a quick moment to survey what we have left, and it depresses the hell out of me. Not counting the Dilaudid, we have maybe twenty (20) tabs of mescaline, five (5) amyls, one-quarter of a salt shaker of cocaine, one (1) sheet of blotter acid, the gallon of Motherfucker (which I'd forgotten about), six (6) beers, a half full bottle of ether, half a brick of weed, forty (40) crank pills and twenty (20) Vicodins. We can still get things going with this, but we might need to stop off somewhere to get more supplies. I already miss the whiskey.

"What's taking you so long?!" my attorney screams. "I'm in pain!"

I come around to his side of the car with the needle. I'm tempted to just stick him with it, make him muscle it, but it'll only make him worse when he comes down and we don't have anymore Dilaudid. Just let him have the rest of it and be quiet for as long as possible.

I tie off his arm again, and he looks away. He needs the needle, but he doesn't dare watch me use it. I find his vein, and I pierce it, pressing down the plunger all the way. He smiles and closes his eyes in a state of utter bliss.

"This is the last of it," I say. "When it wears off, I don't want to hear you whining about it."

"We still have the Vicodin," he mumbles. "That will hold me over until the sixth circle. I know a guy there."

It occurs to me that maybe I should take the Gerber away from him, but it is nestled between both of his hands like a talisman. There's no way I can pry it away from his grip.

Never mind. I throw the needle into the desert and go back to the trunk. I'm running out of options. I don't want to waste the crank and coke and amyls. We'll need them later for our battle with Nixon. But I'm not sure that I want downers now. I mull it over while chugging two of the beers. Fuck it. The mescaline will keep me alert and watchful. And why not get into the Motherfucker a little? Not much. Not so much that the rat poison gets to me.

I down a couple of tabs of mescaline with a shot's

worth of Motherfucker. Great Jesus God! I almost spit it out, but I'm a professional. I swallow that vile garbage and wonder at how anyone can stand this shit.

But they say the second drink always goes down smoother. I take another belt, just to see if the old saying is true, and it is not. Not by anyone's standards. My cheeks balloon out, but my lips remain sealed. It takes me two swallows to get the swill down.

I collapse into the driver seat, and it takes me a moment to get my head straight. My attorney moans in his sleep, but everything else is quiet on this drag. Quiet until I rev the engine and throw it into gear. We jump forward like a springing mountain lion. My heart races, but my attorney doesn't move except to rub his considerable belly.

How much more desert do we have to drive through? O Lord, when will we get our chance at Nixon? I'm chomping at the bit. I smell blood, and I want to slay the fucker. How many more circles do we have to brave? I forget, did Dante mention nine or ten? No, wait. There are officially nine circles. The tenth isn't really a circle. It's the center of Hell, where Satan lives with three heads. In the left and right mouths are Brutus and Cassius respectively. In the middle mouth is Judas Iscariot. Eerie.

If that's the kind of people who live in Satan's mouth, who lives in his asshole? Grim. Best not to think on it.

I think I need some Motherfucker. Not that it tastes great, but a man develops a fondness for that poison. I pull over so I can get the gallon jug. As an afterthought, I grab the Vicodin. My attorney is going to need them when he wakes up. Best not to have another ugly scene.

5

Politicians and pedophiles. Decadent Romans. I must shoot something. Honest Abe. Carcosa. Ye fucking gods! Don't step into that vagina.

An hour later my attorney stirs. He starts moaning slightly, and he lets loose a wretched fart evil enough to be named and given a Social Security number. He's coming out of it, and it hasn't been very long. Already his body is building up a resistance. But this time I know he has the Gerber. And I have Vicodin. I'll probably have to feed him six pills, but this will make a difference.

About fifteen minutes later he opens his eyes. He blinks, confused, like a bear coming out of hibernation. "Where are we?" he mumbles.

"I think this is the sixth circle," I say. "What is this place reserved for?" Trying to keep his mind off the dope.

He stretches out and lets his head fall over the headrest. Gazing up at the devil red sky. "It's for politicians and pedophiles. Down here, they're the same goddam thing."

"Jesus. That's a heavy thing."

"Sure is." He starts scratching his arms like a fiend. Jesus. The drug still has him.

"You feeling all right?" I ask.

"I need Dilaudid," he says.

"We're out. I told you."

"I can get more. I said I know a guy. Where's the Vicodin?"

I give him the bottle. "Only take four. Any more than that, and you'll be a gibbering millstone around my neck."

He takes six, just like I thought he would. Good. Maybe we're not as fucked as I think we are. We can do this. I can keep him on a leash. He wraps the pills in a handkerchief and crushes them with the bottle of Motherfucker. Then he carefully opens the handkerchief over his mouth and gets every crumb in. He washes it all down with some Motherfucker, and then he starts licking the handkerchief. When he's satisfied that he's gotten every bit of those pills, he takes another swig of Motherfucker and swishes it through his mouth before swallowing. He lets out a tremendous sigh and contentedly rests back.

"So. You know a guy?"

"Mm-hm." Not even opening his eyes. The poor brute can't even form words, can he?

"Can he get us more Turkey?" I ask. "We ran out a while ago."

"He can get us anything. Do you want a slave boy? Maybe a sex slave boy?"

"Jesus shit! What's wrong with you?! No, I don't want a sex slave boy. Do I look like a decadent Roman to you?"

"All white people look like decadent Romans to me," he says. "But if you wanted a sex slave boy, he could get it for you."

It. Not even he. Things have spiraled out of control. I need to relax, but none of the drugs we have on hand will do that for me. Sure, the weed would help, but the only thing that can calm me down comes in the form of gunpowder. I must shoot something. Immediately. I stomp on the brake and yank us over to the side of the road.

"What are you doing?" my attorney asks.

I ignore him. There are still some dead soldiers in the backseat. I grab all of them and stalk off into the desert. What I would give for high powered explosives right now. I need some Tannerite at the very least. How many teeth would a canister of that stuff cost?

This desert is completely featureless. There's nothing to shoot at, so I throw up one of the empties and draw down on it. My aim is horribly off, but the sound of the gun firing is enough to make me feel better. My second shot blows my target off the ground.

When I throw the next one up, I blow it to pieces with one shot. I keep going until I run out of ammo, so I reload and I continue until I'm out of targets and out of breath. I pant, feeling the booze sweat pouring down my forehead and back.

Success. I reload and head back to the car. My attorney looks blankly at me, but I think he understands now. Despite his race, we are still of the same ilk. He understands the need for sudden explosions.

I drop down into my seat. "Can your guy get us some Tannerite?"

"He can get us an atom bomb. If we have enough teeth, that is. We have a lot, but not nearly enough for that kind of thing."

"We won't need it," I say. "We have all we need to defeat Nixon. We will march on a road of bones."

My attorney grins. "Keep going straight. In a while we'll come upon a hut on the right. That's where we need to go."

"Right." I stomp on the accelerator. We're getting this done for good or ill.

An hour later I finish off the Motherfucker and throw the bottle out onto the road. By then my attorney had taken four more Vicodin, and I start to wonder where the hell this hut is. We're running low on drugs, to say nothing of fuel for the shark, and my paranoia is setting in. Not quite a full fledged Fear, but we're getting there. I'm getting tempted to pull over and see what else I can get from the trunk to self medicate, but then I see it at the crest of the next hill.

"We're here," I tell my attorney.

He cracks his eyes open and peers into the distance. "That's it, all right. Pull up behind it and park so we can't be seen from the road. We have to be careful in these grim and dangerous times."

Too true. I pull off the road and park as close to the hut as I can. It looks bigger now that I'm next to it. From faraway, it looked like it could have been the type of thing Herman Melville would have lived in during his Typee years. Up close it looks like a suburban home.

"As your attorney I advise you to let me do the talking. But first I'll need some of the cocaine."

We go to the trunk, and he is dismayed when he sees how little we have left. This doesn't stop him from finishing off the salt shaker and dropping it back into the trunk. For later. We then go around the hut to the front door. My attorney pauses, thinking, his fist raised halfway in the air. His head rocks back and forth, and then he stiffens up.

"Right. That's it," he says. Then he knocks twice, rapid fire, and three more times spaced out. The last knock is a light tap. He backs up and waits.

An unseen intercom goes off with a static sound. Then a robot voice comes at us like a ninja in the dark: "Who goes?"

"It's me," my attorney says. "I need a few things. I have teeth."

"Who is your companion? Is he a pig?"

"No, of course not. He's my client. I would never ratfuck you, man."

"I wanna hear him say it."

My attorney nods at me. I say, "I'm not a pig. Fuck them. They're swine, and if I had any leeches, I'd put them on them."

The door creaks open, and in the slight crack I can see a hulking beast of a man, bigger than my attorney. He wears an eye patch and has a scant beard sliced through with scar tissue. One of his hands holds some kind of hook. No. Wait. His hand *is* the hook. Jesus. What has my attorney gotten me into?

"Come in," the stranger says.

My attorney enters first, and he clasps hands with the stranger. They clap each others backs. When I enter, I can see him more clearly. He looks very familiar. I shake his hand, and his grip is firm and strong but not overpowering. I've met many US presidents, and they all have the same handshake.

Holy shit. The dots connect, and I know who this man is. Of course. This circle is for politicians, and though we know him as Honest Abe, Lincoln is still a politician, for good or ill.

He sees my recognition. He tries to smile, but it's too crooked and broken by cynicism. "Yes, yes, I'm Lincoln. Never mind that. What can I get for you?"

"How did you get into this snake pit?" I ask. "If any president was bound for the other place, I would surely think it was you. You and poor, dumb Jimmy Carter."

"Yes, I'm a politician," he says, "but I was also a pedophile."

Blasphemy! The greatest US president in history can't be a pedophile! Is nothing sacred in this world?

"It was a slave boy," he says. "When I was a young lawyer in Springfield, I encountered him. He delivered a letter to me from his master down South. As soon as I saw him, I had to have him. Twelve was a different kind of age back then. It came with more knowledge of the world. But he was willing. I was able. I feel bad about it now, all things considered, but pedophilia can't be undone. So here I am."

I look to my attorney. He shrugs. "He can get things. So he likes 'em young. *I* like 'em young. Maybe not *that* young, but still."

A pit of snakes, indeed. I'm not going to let my guard down around these animals. It might not be a good gesture to have my gun out and ready for action, but I'm going to certainly touch the butt the whole time. They will not get the drop on me.

My attorney starts to barter over the price of a giant

hunk of heroin. I've never seen a bigger bag of the rotten stuff, but he gets it at a good price, I think. We also load up on more drugs for me: a handle of Wild Turkey 101, more Motherfucker, a brick of cocaine, some hashish, more acid and something else. I don't catch the name right away, but then he says it again: Carcosa. It sounds familiar. Maybe something from Bierce.

"It's some real end of the world shit," Lincoln says. "I only recommend doing it once. It will change you. You will see things that no man was meant to see. Real Cthulhu type shit."

My attorney says, "We'll take six of them."

"It's freaky," Lincoln says. "I don't recommend you take more than one each."

"We're professionals. We'll take ten."

Jesus. He exchanges teeth for our new drug collection, and I cart it all out to our kit in the trunk of the shark. I organize it quickly so everything is easy to find, even if we're twisted out of our minds. I glance back and see that my attorney is bullshitting with Lincoln like they're lifelong buddies. They laugh and shake hands. Lincoln tips a salute in my direction, but I don't return the gesture. At this rate we'll learn that Atticus Finch is really a racist. That's a heavy one, but it fits.

My attorney approaches, and I think he's ready to cook up and start the injections. But no, when he reaches into the trunk, he takes out the baggie of Carcosa. "I've heard about this shit ever since I died. We have to do this right away. As your attorney, I advise you to chew on this." He hands me a lump of something that looks and smells slightly like shit.

"Maybe this is a bad idea," I say.

He pops one into his mouth and chews for a full minute. When he swallows, he grimaces and nearly hacks out the Carcosa. "It goes down rough, but don't puke it up. If you puke it up, you won't get the full effects."

Shit. Buy the ticket, take the ride. The going is already

weird. Why not turn pro? I stick the lump of Carcosa into my mouth, and the taste is wretched. I don't want to have this thing on my tongue, much less chew it for so goddam long. I hold my nose, but it doesn't help. I force myself to chew, and it's tough like the best beef jerky. After what seems like years, I finally get the bugger down. It leaves a slimy trail all the way down my throat. I cough, trying to clear it out, but it sticks like glue.

"The first wave is horrible," my attorney says. "It might be better to not drive right now. But when the second wave hits, we should be good to go."

Nothing is happening. Maybe Lincoln ripped us off. If so, I'd go back in that hut and pistol whip him to within an inch of his life. "Do you feel anything?"

"Not a goddam thing," my attorney says. He takes off his sunglasses and wipes at his face. When he opens his eyes, I see that they have three lobes. I blink, thinking it's a mirage, but it's still there.

"Are you feeling all right?" I ask. "You don't look so hot."

My attorney's facial hair is turning into tentacles, and they waver about his face, seeking prey. "I'm fine, but you look like shit, man. Literally. Your skin's brown and mottled, and you're shriveling into an amorphous shape."

Amorphous. *Amorphous.* AMORPHOUS! My attorney is not paid by the word, and I'm certain the dumb brute doesn't know that one. Did that word come from my own mind?

The bats overhead are now larger and man shaped but with no faces. They howl and screech like warriors. The desert floor is now a sea of waving dunes, and the scant dead trees are clawing hands, demons trying to break out of Hell. Wait, that makes no sense in this place. Is there somewhere worse than Hell?!

"I have the Fear!" I scream.

"It's OK," my attorney says. "It's not real. It's the drug. Just ride it out."

Except now he has a swirling vortex for a mouth, and six arms dance at his sides. His hair looks like a dying squid, and he is suddenly blotted out by a heavy shadow. I look up and see a giant monster above us. Something like Godzilla by way of deep sea octopi.

"Ye fucking gods! Do you see that thing?!" I cry out.

My attorney looks up. "I think that's Cthulhu."

He *can* see it. This isn't the drugs. This is *real*. We have to get out of here immediately. I grab my attorney's arm, and he screams, pushing away at me.

"Don't grab me like that! I'll fucking shoot your balls off!"

I look down and see that my balls are no longer hidden by my shorts. No, they're growing out of my shorts, and I see them pop off and roll out into the desert. I can't flee now, not without my balls. I rush after them, intent on catching them, but the wind keeps blowing them away. I run for miles, but to no avail. I'm just going to have to accept it. I'm going to spend the rest of my days without balls. Is such a life worth living? Probably not.

I take out my .44 and press it up against my head, angled so that if fired, it will indeed remove the important part of my brain. Can't fuck something like this up, you know.

Cthulhu hunkers down so he can look me in the eyes. He glances at the gun and shakes his head. "That's no way to kill Nixon."

"I have no balls," I say. "I don't want to live without my balls."

"So Nixon wins because you have no balls? That doesn't sound like you. As your lord and savior, I advise you to walk through this door." He points a hoary finger at a door I didn't see before. It's old fashioned with a gilded knob and a keyhole you can actually look through. Nothing holds this door up, and when I peer behind it, it disappears.

"Are my balls in here?" I ask.

"They are. And so much more awaits."

That settles it, then. I open the door and see nothing but darkness. The darkness seems alive, though. It has a pulse. I touch it, and it feels like watery gelatin. A dark tendril slips up my arm like a snake, and even if I wanted to back away, I wouldn't be able to. Might as well succumb to its will. I step into it, and it envelops me like a warm blanket.

"What the fuck are you doing?" my attorney yells. "Don't step into that vagina! You'll never come back."

It doesn't look like a vagina to me. Doesn't feel like one, either. Fuck it. My attorney is on his own Carcosa trip. Let me enjoy mine. I step through, and everything around me goes dark. I hear the door slam shut, and it is gone.

Yes. Buy the ticket, take the ride. But what kind of ride have I bought? What madness lies ahead?

I have the sensation of falling, but I can't see anything, so I can't be sure. I feel the urge to vomit, but I have to keep it together. I have to keep the Carcosa down. This is a once in a lifetime trip, and I need to see it through to the end, for good or ill. Images start flashing as I fall past. A baby struggling its way out of a grotesquely stretched vagina. A child doing terrible things. A teenager doing terrible things. Jesus! It's me! My life is flashing before my eyes! I'm dead again! I'm certain of it!

I see all the drugs and booze, and I see the Kentucky Derby. My beating at the hands of the Hell's Angels. I see Vegas and the campaign trail. All the madness of the 'Eighties. Bill Clinton. Writing and partying and drinking and fucking. It's all there, like a grim specter delivered courtesy of the Ghost of Christmas Past. I don't regret a second of it. At first it's shocking, but as I become used to it, I kind of enjoy it. I fall for decades, reliving all the best and worst parts of my life. I wish I brought whiskey with me. That would have completed this madness. Maybe some acid.

There I am on the phone, and the gun goes to my head. I don't remember this, but it seems right. I always said that when I wasn't having fun anymore, I'd take the Hemingway. "So it goes." Kurt Vonnegut said that, and he was not wrong.

The darkness resumes. Before it made me nervous. Now it annoys me. Maybe I can see the movie of my life again. That would be nice. I wonder if Depp fulfilled my wishes of having my ashes shot out of a cannon. He's a good sort. I like him a lot. But he is Hollywood, and Hollywood can be treacherous. Maybe I'll find out in the ninth circle.

I'm no longer falling. I don't know how I know it, but my gut senses that I'm now just floating in the void. Miles below me I see a spot of light, and I'm not falling but drifting. Drifting toward it. As I get closer, I see it's my own body. Not the one I left on earth with the top of its head missing. No, it's the Hell me, the one with a mission to take down Nixon himself. There is a beatific smile on my face, and my arms are crossed over my chest like some sort of pharaoh of ancient Egypt.

The void stretches me out until I can no longer see me, but I know that I'm drifting toward my Hell flesh. I cross my arms across my chest in the exact image, and I feel myself, balls and all, fitting back into my body like a hand in a glove.

The darkness is gone. The bats remain, flapping through the sky like little missiles. I sit up and look to my attorney, who is resting in the exact same position as I was in moments ago. The hills in the distance are now waving tentacles, so I know the Carcosa still has me in its grip, but I can at least act like the reasonable man that I am.

It's best not to wake him up. It would interrupt the movie of his life, and I'm not going to do that to someone else. Let him come out of it naturally. It might be a good idea to get a few uppers in my system, so I go to the trunk and bury the goddam Carcosa as much as I can. No need to get back into that rotten stuff. I open the brick of cocaine and stick my nose into it like Scarface trying to breathe naturally. My heart races, and it helps distance myself from the Carcosa. I'm feeling more myself now.

My attorney lumbers over. "Did you see that? My life story, man. It was grim stuff."

"As your physician, I advise you to fill your head with as much cocaine as you can." I offer him the brick, and he obeys.

His nostrils are caked white, but his eyes are clearer than I've ever seen them. "That's the ticket, man. Wow, that Carcosa stuff. We can't do that again."

"Indeed." But we're just saying this. We both know we'll suck it down before we reach our destination.

"We need to get going," he says. "We're behind schedule. Let me drive for a while."

I can't argue with that. I grab the bottle of Wild Turkey 101 for company, and we get back into the car. The horizon is still shaky, and the bats still have human heads with no faces, but we can deal with this. We forge ahead, passing the bottle back and forth to even out the cocaine.

Only then do I remember that we forgot to get Tannerite. Shit. So it goes.

6

Dictators and warriors. We need to fix the car. The edge. We have weapons. The tree of liberty. Fear and loathing at the Howard Johnson.

We are halfway through the seventh circle when my attorney pulls us over. He wipes at his nose, which is still powdered. When his fingers are covered with the stuff, he snorts what he can off of them and licks the rest away.

"More coke?" I ask.

"No, it's not that. We're going to be in the eighth circle

soon. Do you know about the savages who live there?"

"You're my Virgil."

He squints his eyes at me. "I don't fuck guys."

Of all the references he doesn't get so far, it's the Dante reference. Or maybe he's doing this on purpose. I know he's familiar with Dante's work. How could he not know Virgil? He's fucking with me. I know it. The swine.

"It's all the dictators and warriors in history," he says. "None of them were good in the end, so they all ended up here. The eighth circle is a goddam battlefield, and we'll never make it through the way we are now. We need to fix the car."

"Fix it? There's nothing wrong with it."

He shakes his head. "You haven't been down here for very long. We're going to have to visit an armory. Luckily, I know a guy."

"You know a lot of guys down here."

"It's not going to be cheap, but he's a friend. I can jew him down to a good price."

It's been a while since I heard that phrase. Up in the living world, no one would have stood for that kind of talk. Hell is a different place, and it makes a savage even more savage. There is no edge down here, or if there is, we're all on it.

"Do what you think is best," I say. "Before we do that, though, I'm going into the trunk. You need anything?"

"The hash. I feel in the mood for hash."

I go in the back and fill a pipe with the hashish for my attorney. For myself, I grab what remains of the weed. It is moving in my hand like some kind of sea weed. Jesus God! When, O Lord? When will the Carcosa be done with me?

I roll a joint and start back to the passenger seat. I glance into the backseat and remember the dog for the first time in a while. Maybe I should get some Motherfucker for him. But he's not moving. I go in for a closer look, and it's not breathing at all. I poke it in the ribs, and it doesn't react.

"Shit," I say. "I think the dog is dead."

"Impossible," my attorney says. He turns in his seat and slaps the shit out of the dead dog. It does not yelp, exactly as I expected.

"Maybe we should have fed him," I say.

"He's pretending," my attorney says. Now he's on his knees in the front seat, and he's throttling the dog with one hand and slapping it with the other. "Wake up, you piece of shit! Wake up!"

Nothing.

"Forget it," I say. "Patches is dead. Let's find a place to bury him and just move on."

My attorney snarls, showing off all of his teeth. "No. We're going to hold on to the bastard. We can still use it against Nixon. Maybe not as a threat, but more as a way to show we mean business."

I don't think I like this way of thinking, but Patches is dead. I don't think he'll have a problem with it. Fuck it. I let it go and hand over the hash pipe. My attorney lights it and takes in a lungful.

"Yes. That hit the spot."

I light up my own joint, and I feel the Carcosa backing down a bit. The tentacles in the distance no longer look real. They're more like a bad CGI effect in a shitty movie. It feels good to mellow out a little.

"We're almost to my guy," my attorney says. "It's in a town, and we might need to stay overnight while he works on the car."

"As long as we can afford it," I say. "How many teeth does one room go for?"

"We've got plenty. We'll probably be broke by the time we leave here, but we'll be ready for anything that gets in our way."

"Fine," I say. "Who lives in *this* circle? Anything we need to worry about?"

"No, just a bunch of anarchists. People who took it too

far and shot up a school or blew up something important. I hear bin Laden is down here somewhere."

"This is grim."

"Yes. But *we* have weapons."

Indeed.

After driving for another hour, my attorney takes a side road, and we find ourselves driving through the middle of a small town. Ramshackle buildings lean on groaning skeletons, begging to slump and die. Derelict gas stations loom above us like stone giants, forgotten by time and God. Gun shops are everywhere, as are pawn stores, but no one loiters around them. The only sound is the rumble of the shark.

"Is there no one alive in this town?" I ask.

"They're here," my attorney says. "They're just hiding. They don't like it when strangers ride through."

"I thought you said you know these people."

"I know *a guy.*"

Right. I take out my .44, but I know that if they're hiding from us, these people are more scared of us than we are of them. I don't expect action, but I'm ready for it if it happens.

We pull into a weedy parking lot, which is empty except for what might be a Ford Maverick. I haven't seen one in ages, but I see that it casts no shadow. There is something not real about it, like it might be alive. I have a bad feeling in my guts. "Don't park next to that thing," I say.

"As your attorney, I advise you to not worry about it. Yes, it's a monster, but it won't bother us unless we fuck with it." He whips his sunglasses off and stares at me with menace. "You're not going to fuck with it, are you?"

"Jesus God no!"

He parks on the opposite side of the lot from the Maverick. It turns its headlights on us, but it doesn't act. It's just curious about us. I pretend to ignore it as my attorney leads the way to what looks like a broken down body shop. His ham fist bangs mercilessly at the door.

"I hear you!" someone says. "Stop fucking hammering at my goddam door! I've got a hangover and a need to murder someone!"

My hand tightens on my gun, but my attorney shakes his head. "He doesn't mean it." But my attorney has eased his Gerber out. This does not fill me with confidence.

The door opens, and I see another familiar face that I can't quite place. He looks like a geek trying to play himself off as a tough guy. My attorney shakes hands with him. "Good to see you, man."

"Long time no see," the stranger says. "What do you need?"

My attorney starts listing a bunch of gibberish, pointing at our car. I only catch some words because they're related to weaponry. Things like machine guns and grenade shooters. This has gotten heavy for us. Very heavy. I'm glad I'm recording all of this for history.

The stranger takes notes. About halfway through, he holds up a finger. "This is going to cost a lot of teeth."

My attorney flashes a bag full of Hell's Angels' teeth. "I can pay your price."

The stranger seems more eager to help now. He scribbles his notes faster like a peasant who is excited to help his king. When the exchange is done, they settle on a price. My attorney pays it.

"How long will this take?" he asks.

"Tomorrow morning," the stranger says. "Come by, and I'll have everything ready for you."

"OK," my attorney says. "We're going to stay at the Howard Johnson down the block. If you need anything, you let me know."

And then it comes to me. The stranger. "Timothy McVeigh," I say.

The stranger grins. "You a fan?"

"No. You're a swine of the first order. Execution was

too kind for the savage likes of you. They should have had you drawn and quartered and thrown to the goddam dogs."

"Hey, I know you. You're that gonzo journalist. You were kind of an inspiration to me, what with your drive to bring the truth to the people. I brought the truth to the people by exposing how wrong the government was with the Waco showdown and the Ruby Ridge thing. The tree of liberty must be refreshed from time to time—"

"—with the blood of patriots and tyrants. I know my history. I don't need to learn it from a geek like you. I should Mace you and throw you to the sodomites."

"Calm down," my attorney says. "No need to fight. We're gentlemen here and professionals. Mr. McVeigh has services he can render to us, and we have the payment he requires. Let's be friends or at least businessmen."

"You run in the same circles with a lot of scum," I say.

My attorney turns to McVeigh. "I apologize for my client. He's very passionate about certain things."

"Just keep a leash on him," McVeigh says, "and we should be fine."

I reach for my can of Mace, but my attorney stops me and drags me out of the body shop. He's stronger than I am in a normal state, but I think a few amyls and some crank can turn the tides.

"Relax, man. He's paid the price for what he's done."

"He's a killer of children," I say. "That's a hole you just can't dig out of."

"Everyone who ends up in this circle gets castrated before they're released into the wild. Timothy McVeigh has no cock and balls down here, just a smooth spot where hair can never grow back. Imagine spending the rest of your unlife with no equipment down there."

I think back to my Carcosa trip, and it makes me feel a little better about dealing with scum. Not much, but a little. I'm OK with letting this go.

We head for the Chevy, and I get into the trunk for our drug kit. I'm tempted to leave the Carcosa behind, but we're not going anywhere today. If we get into that rotten stuff, then who cares? I take the baggie and put it in with the other drugs.

"Take the dog, too," my attorney says.

"No. The dead dog stays."

"This town is full of savages. They might steal the dog. For reasons."

I don't want to know what these reasons are, but being a reasonable sort, I compromise. "Let's put the dog in the trunk, then. No one will find it there."

My attorney wants to argue, but he knows when I'm putting my foot down. "Sure. OK."

I put Patches in the trunk. I know that when we get the car back, there is going to be a terrible stink back there. I don't think we should put our drug collection in there when the time comes. That might not be so bad. At least we won't have to pull over to get to the drugs in the future. Especially if my attorney is right about the next circle.

Just before we begin the short trek to the Howard Johnson, my attorney peeks in the kit and pulls out a sheet of blotter acid. He tears it in two and gobbles down one half. He grimaces as he forces the whole thing down. He then hands the remaining half to me.

Why not? I ball it up and shove it in my mouth. I suck on it for a while before I start chewing. It goes down hard, so I help it along with a couple of shots of Wild Turkey 101. My attorney motions for the bottle, so I give it to him. He takes a couple of belts down, too.

"You make a hell of a doctor," he says.

I take the bottle back. "I wouldn't have gotten this far without you as my attorney."

"I think we should wait for the acid to kick in before we try getting our room."

"That's a horrible idea. But it sounds like a good

challenge. Let's do this."

There is a bar a block down from the Howard Johnson, so we get a booth and a few drinks to wait for the rush of hallucinogens. A tooth gets us a pitcher of Motherfucker, and we polish it off pretty quickly. We're just about ready to order another when I see the pitcher has become an empty skull. I smell it, and I determine that it's a Celtic skull. Probably murdered by an English swine. I check to see if there are British blade marks on the base, but I can't find anything.

The bartender approaches. His face is also a skull, and he's grinning at us. "Can I get anything else for you fellas?"

Jesus! How can he talk without lips?! Better to let my attorney handle this.

He says, "I think we're good. When did your head turn into a snake?"

The bartender's skull shifts slightly. I don't see a snake. But the skull looks like it might be a reptile's. Maybe. Yes. He's got a forked tongue. It flicks out and licks the empty sockets where there should be eyes.

"I think we're ready to check in," I say.

My attorney nods and turns to the bartender. "Thank you for your help. We'll manage from here."

We stagger out to the street, which has become a conveyor belt. Cars pass by, but none of them are moving of their own free will. Their tires are all hands, and they're gripping the belt for dear life. The sky is pure red, and I can feel cancer growing all over me. I look down at my arms, and I can see melanomas oozing out of my flesh.

Relax. It's just the drug. The melanomas aren't real.

"I don't see them," my attorney says.

I have to get a grip. I don't need him poking around in my goddam brain.

"I'm not poking into anything. You're mumbling, man. But now that you mention melanomas, I think I have a few growing over here."

I give him a once over, and he's wrong. There aren't melanomas growing on him; he is one big cancer lump in an Acapulco shirt. Dear Lord, this trip is turning on me. I have to keep this under control.

We come closer to the Howard Johnson, except it's no longer a hotel. It's an Aztec ziggurat, and they're chopping out the hearts of slaves at the top and throwing the goddam organs down on us. It's raining hearts. They plop on the pavement all around us, leaving awful red marks wherever they bounce. My attorney grabs one in midair and chomps into it like it's an apple.

"What are you doing?!" I scream. "Are we resorting to cannibalism already?!"

"Stop jabbering," he says. "We need to play it cool."

"Jabbering?! You just ate a human heart!"

"A human heart?" He looks at his hand, which is filmed over with blood. He licks it. "Tastes like pomegranate to me."

It's the drug. It's got to be the drug. I can't fight it. If I fight it, it will fight me. And it *will* win. Just ride this out. We're going to be fine.

We enter the ziggurat, and the Aztec clerk is wearing a living Quetzalcoatl, wavering around his shoulders and neck. He says something. I think it might be Spanish.

My attorney responds, also in Spanish. Maybe he's not a Samoan after all. I'll have to file that away for later. They barter for a while, and my attorney gets the key to the room.

In the elevator, he curses and slams his fist into the wall. "Where is my .357, goddammit?!"

Then I remember I took his gun away. For his own good. I don't think now is a good time to mention that. "What did the clerk say?"

"We can have the room, but we have to evict the lowlifes who are in it right now. They're a week late on their rent, so we can use whatever means necessary. I can do it with the Gerber, but I'd rather have the .357."

"Oh. Is that all? You dropped it in the lobby. I was going to give it to you in the room, but here." I pull it out from my belt and hand it over.

"Thanks." He gets a tearful look in his eyes. "You're the best friend I've ever had. Thank you so much, man. I love you."

We embrace, and I can feel his giant wet face pressed against my shoulder. Oddly enough, I love the brute right back. We've had our differences, but he's one of the few people I've ever known who could handle life on the Edge.

We get out on the sixth floor. Our room is sixty-six, and the number makes me perk up. I'm not the religious sort, but that number holds a lot of power. I think we're going to have a rough time claiming the room. I have the .44 still, but I'm glad I brought the Extractor, too. Hey, why not? If we have to bust some heads, we might as well get some teeth out of the bargain, right?

We pause in front of the door. My attorney is so good at cop knock that I let him hammer away.

"Fuck off!" the voice on the other side of the door says. "We're busy getting our dicks wet!"

"FBI!" my attorney roars. "We're here to arrest you on charges of pedophilia!"

"And we're sending you to prison!" I shout. "We've measured the erect cocks of all of our inmates, and we've chosen the biggest they've got to be your cellmates! Ron Jeremy looks tiny compared to these men! And they are men. Men who have needs."

"Wait!" The door cracks open, and a sneering geek looks back at us. "You've got the wrong circle of Hell. We're not pedophiles."

My attorney pistol whips him, sending him reeling. I kick open the door, and we charge in. There are two naked teenagers in here, both boys. It takes me a moment to recognize them as Eric Harris and Dylan Klebold, the pigfuckers behind the Columbine shootings. And they're wearing giant, obscene strap-ons.

There is a third person in the room: a girl. She looks very drugged out, and from what I can see, they were in the midst of getting her naked when we arrived. Her clothes are torn to pieces, but she's still covered. She might be legal, but I doubt it.

"You have no right!" Eric, the un-pistol whipped one, says.

"This is our room now," my attorney says. "We can shoot you dead where you stand."

"You don't understand. We've been losers our entire lives. This is our first chance to do something. I've never gotten my dick wet before." He waves the dildo back and forth.

My attorney shoots him in the crotch. He screams and collapses, clutching his ruined pelvis in both bloody hands. Pieces of rubber dick rain down on us.

"There," my attorney says. "Now your dick is wet. Get out of here before I finish you off."

Dylan tries to stand, but his teeth are dribbling down his chin. He tries to pick them up, but my attorney clobbers him again. More teeth go flying. Dylan cries on the floor, probing his mouth to see how many teeth he's lost.

"Don't pick them up," my attorney says. "Just go. And take your shithead friend with you."

Dylan, his eyes wide and already puffing out, struggles to get to his feet. He pulls up Eric, who can barely stand, and the two of them shuffle out of the room, leaving the girl behind. My attorney slams the door shut and bolts it.

"Good riddance," he mumbles. Then he sits down next to the girl. "Baby, did those guys hurt you?"

I don't like the sound of this. I think maybe I shouldn't have given him the gun back. Things are about to get ugly.

"They were going to rape me," she whispers. I can hear

the hurt and fear in her voice.

"We're not going to rape you," my attorney says. "We're professionals. I'm a lawyer, and this is my client. We're on a secret mission. A drug dealer ripped us off, and we're going into the eighth circle to rip his goddam throat out. Here, this will help." He hands her some of the blotter acid. I didn't know he'd pocketed some of it.

"What is this?" she asks.

"Medicine. Chew on it for a while and swallow it down. It will do you good."

"Wait a minute," I say. "That's a bad idea."

My attorney casts his dead gaze at me. "Relax. I'm not going to hurt her." He brushes his hands through her hair and caresses her cheek. "She's beautiful. I would never harm someone so beautiful."

"She looks like she's fifteen," I say. "How old are you, miss?"

"I don't know," she mumbles. "I'm not feeling good. I need medicine." So she ingests the acid my attorney gave her.

"Good girl," he says. Again, he caresses her cheek.

I pull my .44, but I don't point it at anything. "We're in this deep enough as it is. I can't have you molesting a fifteen-year-old girl."

"I'm not molesting her," he says. "I love her." His eyes look slitted, like a snake's. The room is suddenly hotter than ever, and I can feel my clothes sticking to me unnaturally.

"She's a scared little girl," I say. "We don't need this. We should take her down to the lobby. Maybe to the Hell pigs. I don't know."

"It's not illegal down here, man. It's just . . . it's just love." He leans in to kiss her.

"Illegal has nothing to do with it," I say. "This is vile, even for you." To emphasize the point, I cock the hammer. I still don't point the gun, though.

My attorney's face contorts into a postcard picture of

agony. "Why are you doing this? Can't you see I love this girl? It was meant to be!"

"If you touch her with your ape hands, I will put you down like the beast you are. The drugs are taking hold. Just go take a cold shower. Or better yet, a bath. I'll have some grapefruit sent up to us."

He looks to her, and his eyes are filled with tears. His cheeks shine with them. "I finally find love, and this is what happens? Man, this is horrible. This is the end. I can't take this anymore. I'm going into the bathroom to slit my wrists. I hope you're happy."

My attorney goes into the bathroom, and I hear water pouring immediately. The girl looks to me, tears in her own eyes. "Where is he going? He's such a nice man. He saved me from those rapists."

"You're in a rough spot," I say. "Here, let me escort you down to the lobby. They'll know what to do with you there."

"Why is your head shaped like a bat?" she asks.

"Never mind that. The drugs are working. That's all you need to know. You'll see some weird shit before it's through with you, but you're going to be OK."

I bring her down to the clerk, and by then she can't maintain any sense of balance. She keeps recoiling at things that aren't there, at least not at first. Her reactions are feeding my trip, and as soon as she shudders at something, I see a lizard materialize out of nowhere. Sometimes it has wings, sometimes it's more of a snake.

The clerk is made of scales, but his eyes are a normal human being's. This time. I bring her up to the desk and have her lean on it. "For your own safety," I say.

She glances up at the ceiling as if watching a movie unfold. She is awed. Acid will do that to you, at least on your first trip. I've had more trips than an average man can handle, and it's been a long time since I felt like a virgin.

"We stomped on the swine," I tell the clerk. "Those

rapists will never forget what happened to them today. So the room is ours, but we have their victim on our hands." I hook a thumb at the girl.

"Is she a problem?" the clerk asks.

"Damn right she is. We're not pederasts. We don't need this kind of shit weighing us down. Is there someone who can take care of her? The devils have her wasted on acid and God knows what else."

"She's our most popular whore," the clerk says.

I want to pistol whip him, but where's the good in that. You can change a system, but you can't change a way of life. Not without bloody murder. "My attorney and I are not the kind of men who play with girls barely old enough to bleed. You'll have to take her elsewhere. Or maybe I should escort her to a social service."

The clerk chuckles. "You're in Hell. There are no social services down here."

I Mace him on goddam principle. He screams, clawing at his eyes, trying to find the lung space to breathe. He doesn't find any, and I don't help him out. I smack him in the mouth with the Extractor. Most of the teeth are completely shattered, but I pick up a few of them. For later.

I turn to the girl. "Do you have a mother? A family member? Anyone who cares about you?"

The clerk screams through a mouthful of blood, but neither of us pay him mind. "That man. Your attorney. I'm in love with him. He has the nicest spinal column I've ever seen."

Jesus. She's far beyond gone. "You need to come down from the acid. Come here."

She approaches me with a seductive smile, as if I've just offered to lay her, but I lead her to a closet. I push her in, and I lock the door. She utters some kind of protest that I can barely hear.

"This is for your own good," I say. "I'll be back when the acid wears off."

She screams, but that's none of my business. I go back up to our room, and I lock and bolt the door behind us. There are some crazy bastards in this building, and I want to make sure the only one I have to deal with is my batshit crazy attorney. He is still in the bathroom, and I feel like a joint would cool me out a bit. However, when I see the drug kit, it's been ripped to pieces. Dear Jesus, almost all of it is gone. I still have cocaine and the amyls and the crank, but nothing else remains except for half of the whiskey and one-quarter of the Motherfucker. Has my attorney done everything? Even the Carcosa?

I slam my fist against the bathroom door. "Are you in there, you inveterate cocksucker?! Open up!"

A mumbled response: "It's open."

Sure enough it is. When I walk in I see that the bathroom is an abattoir, except with shit and cum in addition to blood. There are bodily fluids all over this room, a crime scene investigator's wet dream. I don't need a blue light to see the madness that this room has become because of my attorney.

His head is in the toilet. At first I think he's dead, but his feet start scrabbling for some kind of grip on the linoleum floor. His hands flail, and I know he's lost all control of himself. I yank his head out of the toilet and drop him on the floor. Face down, so he doesn't choke on any vomit he may have left in him.

"You goddam animal!" I roar. "You did all of the drugs! Why?!"

He mumbles something, but I can't hear it.

"What?! Take the marbles out of your goddam mouth and speak like a man!"

"You took her away from me," he says. "I'm in love with her, but you stole her from me. Did you sodomize her after you left?"

"No! You brute! She's too young for the likes of us. I did not penetrate her in any way!"

His watery, doomed eyes look up at me. Puke still

glistens on his fat lips. "Why did you take her from me? We're going to be married in the spring. I'm going to have kids with her. Maybe even grandkids."

"Stop your gibberish! You're clearly out of your mind!"

He starts crying, and he pushes his face into his meaty hands. Tears start oozing through his fingers and down his forearms. "I can't live without her! You have to kill me! It's the honorable thing!"

"I'm not going to kill you," I say. "I need your help. We have to take down Nixon. Or have you forgotten?"

He takes his hands away from his face, and everything below his nose is covered in stringy snot. "Take that fucking .44 I gave you and finish me off. Blow my fucking brains out. I know you want to. You've never liked me. That's why you stole her from me."

"Nonsense. I'm not going to kill you, and I like you fine. You've ingested a lot of drugs. I don't know if you're going to come out of it, but you have to ride it out. Stay here for a while. Let the drugs work through your system. You'll be fine tomorrow. Just get some sleep. God knows you took enough downers to get there."

He snarls and reaches for his waist. He must have lost his weapons because there's nothing for him to find. "If you don't kill me, I'm going to kill you."

"Not likely. You just relax. Ride it out. Don't move. Just close your eyes and go to sleep. We'll talk in the morning."

"I'm going to kill you," he whispers. "I have to."

"I need to get some sleep. You're going to stay in here. If you open this goddam door, I'm going to Mace you with extreme prejudice. Do you want that kind of action? *Do you?*"

He breaks down and starts weeping. "Go to sleep," he says. "I won't bother you. I know you'd Mace me like the savage that you are."

"It's under my pillow," I say, "so don't test me."

"I won't." He says it like he doesn't mean it. In that moment, I know I won't get any sleep. I'll spend the rest of this night as alert as possible, my finger on the sprayer. Maybe even on the trigger of my .44. I wouldn't use the Extractor on him. Goddammit, I'm still a human being.

I back out of the room, looking into his rock solid eyes. They track my movements, and I know he's as alert as a predator stalking his prey. I slam the door behind me, and I pile a bunch of furniture up against it. I hear him raging and roaring in the bathroom, but he never makes it to the door, not even to rattle the knob. No, he's in a terrible place. He won't be able to do anything until the drugs wear off.

I get into bed, and like I thought I cannot get to sleep. I smoke some hash, but it only makes me paranoid. I keep the Mace in my hand, ready for anything.

But nothing happens.

7

A killing machine. The mysterious button. The pigs at the gate. The battle to end all battles. I will fight no more forever.

I wake up early the next day, but my attorney is already alert and ready to face the trials and tribulations to come. He has ordered breakfast for the both of us, and his eyes are clear. The drugs have worked their way out of his system, and he seems to be on top of himself. I don't need to Mace him. This will be a good day.

I down some OJ and start working on my scrambled eggs and toast. His mouth is caked with the food he's already ingested. Smeared egg white and crumbs of toast and bacon. It's almost like his nose is running all over his lower face. It's disgusting, but I'm hungry and ignore the whole mess.

"Are you ready for today?" he asks. His mouth is full

of food, and I can barely understand him.

"We're locked and loaded. I don't see us having a problem."

"Hell has been a cake walk so far," he continues. "This next circle is no joke. We're going to have to stomp skulls, man. The dictators and warriors are fucking animals. We have to be worse than them. Do you think you can be worse than Stalin?"

Jesus. That's a heavy question. I guess I have to be. "Maybe we should do all of the uppers we have left," I say.

"No. We'll need them for Nixon. This is the last place I know of that we can score good drugs. No one else can help us."

There is a certain finality in his words. I think that maybe we should get some good drugs before we continue. Maybe Tim McVeigh can help us.

We pack up our things, and as we prepare to leave the Howard Johnson, I take a look around. I don't remember getting crazy the night before. In fact, I remember being the voice of reason to my attorney's savage ways, but somehow the room got trashed. There is puke everywhere, maybe an inch thick over the shag rug. All of the lamps are broken, and there is a handprint in blood on the wall, smeared so it looks like whoever made it slid down the wall. Did we murder someone last night? I don't know. I prefer not to think about it.

We don't check out, but we leave the key on the clerk's desk and sneak out like thieves with red right hands.

Down the street we see Tim McVeigh sitting outside of his garage on a folding chair, kicking back and puffing at the biggest cigar I have ever seen. Blue smoke surrounds him like a shroud, and he's drinking from a bottle of Motherfucker. I double check to see that we still have ours. I don't want that swine drinking our shit. Fuck him.

"Is it ready?" my attorney asks.

McVeigh breathes out a stream of cancer. "You bet.

Here, let me show you the modifications I've made."

He speaks another language. I don't even know what he's done to the shark. It's very technical, and it involves heavy weaponry. Maybe the trouble is with the translation. I take a sip of whiskey to sharpen my listening skills. I think.

"Get in," my attorney says. Who am I to argue? He says a few more words to McVeigh, and we're back on the road in no time. Soon we're back on the main drag.

"I think we should have a few drinks," I say. "I'm tense, and I don't know why."

"It's possibly the forerunner of the Fear," he says. "You should feel the Fear. We're heading into dangerous territory. As your attorney, I advise you to not take any drugs unless they're uppers. Heavy uppers."

It must be the end times. "Pull over. I need to get into the drug kit."

I look over what we have left, and it isn't much. It might not be enough for us to handle Nixon. I take it to the front seat and ponder it with my attorney.

"You're the doctor," he says. "What do you advise?"

"Let's take a couple of snorts of coke to get our heads on right," I say.

"Good."

We each snort a couple of lines to get our synapses firing off like they should be. Now that I feel better, I see that we should be conserving our efforts. I hand my attorney two amyls and keep a couple for myself before putting the kit in the back seat.

"Don't do them yet," I say. "Wait until we run into trouble. Then we'll be unstoppable."

"I should tell you about the modifications I had done to this car, in case anything happens to me." He slaps the ashtray, and a control panel slides out. There are many buttons, and none of them are labeled.

"Pay attention," my attorney says. He points to each button and tells me what they do. There is a button that will cause the fenders to turn into machine guns. Another will raise up armor that will deflect almost all weaponry. The roof will rise up to protect us, but he does not advise us to do that. We need three-sixty vision, after all. There are other buttons, and one of them will unleash a flamethrower.

But there is one that he doesn't explain. "Tell me," I say. "I have to know. Maybe one of these savages will machete your head off, and what then?"

"No," my attorney says. "This last button is too important. I'll tell you about it if you ever need to know what it does. Pray that never happens."

I keep the amyls close to me. Just in case. You can't be too careful in this goddam snake pit. Right.

About an hour later we come upon a barricade in the road. Pigs mill about, their hands resting on their guns or billy clubs. At first I panic, not wanting any of this action. "Crash through the fuckers!" I scream. "They'll never do a thing to stop us."

"Relax," my attorney says. "These are the good guys. Just play it cool and let me do all the talking."

"Have you turned on me?!" I roared. "We're in the belly of the beast! You can't pull shit like this! You made a deal with the swine! I know, you cocksucker. *I know.*"

"It's not like that. I'm telling you, they're not going to hassle us. Watch and see."

I pull my .44. I'm not going to play around with the savages down here. Memories of the Democratic National Convention in Chicago come back to me. Once you've been tear-gassed, you will never forget it. It's why I wear my shirts. I want to look like a tourist. Tourists are not generally tear-gassed. I see their blackjacks, very much like the Extractor, and I can barely keep my breakfast down. Someone's going to die here. I can feel it in my balls. It might even be me.

My attorney stops at the roadblock, and the king pig looms over the both of us. "Where do you think you two

Fear and Loathing in Hell

are headed?"

"This man is my client," my attorney says. "We need to cross the eighth circle. It's imperative to his job."

"What's his job?" the king pig asks. I see his cohorts eyeing us very carefully. I think I can take out three of them, but the other two will undoubtedly murder us. Yes. I hope my attorney knows what he's doing.

"He's a diplomat," my attorney says. "We can't explain what we're doing, but you have to let us through. More importantly, you never saw us." He winks at the king pig.

The king pig nods. "I see. Do you have any identification?"

"No! Of course not! If we're caught with identification, they'll murder us or worse! They'll use my client as a bargaining chip, and I have no doubt that they'll blow my goddam brains out on principle! Does no one notify you of these things? Do you want to go to court?"

The king pig is immediately chastised. He backs away with his hands crossed in front of him like he expects to get kicked in the nuts. "Sorry, sir. I had no idea."

"That's fine," my attorney says. "Just let us through, and I'll forget the whole thing happened."

"Are you sure you want to go out there?" the king pig asks. "It's very dangerous. There are savages in the eighth circle. I don't know if you can make it through. I only ask because your client is such an important man."

"We'll make it," my attorney says. "I upgraded this car. We'll destroy any poor bastard who crosses our path."

"Good." The king pig even grins at this. "Very good. I'm sorry to have interrupted you. Kyle! Let these people through! They're very important!"

The barricade is removed from the road. My attorney smiles up at the king pig. "You've served us well today. That won't be forgotten."

"Thank you, sir."

My attorney stomps on the petal, and the shark surges

forward so quickly I nearly shit my pants. I look back and the barricade is shrinking swiftly. They all watch after us, and I can swear I can see us in their mirrored aviators getting smaller and smaller until neither of us could see each other.

"This just got serious," my attorney says. "We have to be very watchful. The cocksuckers out here are very dangerous. We'll need to kill anyone we see out here."

This sounds reasonable. I inspect my weapon, and it is greased and loaded and ready to go. I'm almost eager to run into the bastards out here. Maybe we can even collect a few more teeth. I don't know what we'd need them for this far into our journey, but they would be good to have, I think.

A mile down the road we see a hitchhiker. He's an Asian man, short but very thick. Thick with muscle. He carries a sack over his shoulder, and he's dressed in a very old fashioned style. Lots of fur, including a fur hat. He has a Fu Manchu mustache that goes all the way down to his chest. He looks very powerful and very mad.

But he has his thumb extended.

"Let's give this guy a lift," I say.

"No," my attorney says. "We can't pick up anyone out here. They're all dangerous maniacs. I'm getting bad vibes off of him."

"Nonsense. Yes, he looks dangerous. But there isn't a danger in the world that a well placed .44 shot can't fix. We have many guns. He'll be scared shitless of us. But he looks interesting. I need to get a recording of him."

My attorney slows the car down. "All right, but if anything happens, I'm holding you accountable. I will sue you to the fullest extent of the law."

"You'd do that, wouldn't you?"

"In a heartbeat." My attorney dips his finger into the cocaine and manages to get a healthy mountain range balanced on it. He snorts it and licks his powdery finger.

The car stops, and the stranger runs toward us. Without

even touching the car he leaps over the door and eases into the backseat like an acrobatic. "Thank you for the ride." My attorney accelerates.

"What's your name?" I ask. I make sure he sees that the recorder is going.

"Genghis Khan."

"Jesus! Like that movie with John Wayne? *The Conquerer?*"

"Fuck that cracker," Khan says. "He made me look like a joke. You can't believe how many people give me shit over that movie. Although I've gotten very good at removing their heads with my bare hands. You know, drinking out of skulls isn't quite what you'd think. If you're going to do that sort of thing, you want to fill it to the brim, but when you do that it spills out the eyeholes. Unacceptable in my opinion."

"What about eating the hearts of your enemies?" my attorney asks. "That can't be a letdown."

"No. It's very delicious. High in protein."

"You speak very good English for an ancient Mongolian," I say.

"Down here? I've gotten a lot of practice. Hundreds of years is a long time to go without learning anything."

True. Khan is definitely an interesting man. For an ancient ruler he was very open minded. From what I remember he had a habit of making his conquered enemies into highly decorated officials, and he never converted them to his own religion. They were always encouraged to follow their beliefs. Khan gets a bad rap these days, but he did pretty good in his time. Too bad his sons were all fuckups.

"What are you doing all the way out here?" I ask.

"I'm trying to get to the battle. I was knifed by one of my concubines. I thought she was loyal to me. She had great tits, and I'm a huge fan of spreading my seed every chance I get. You know they say that there are a lot of people around today who descended from me? True story.

Anyway, she left me for dead, all in the name of that cocksucker Custer."

"George Armstrong Custer?" I ask.

"Yes. He's been warring with Alexander the Great down here. Custer was the biggest fuckup in history, so naturally I'm with Alexander. I didn't know my concubine was Custer's second cousin. I guess that was stupid on my part. Never again, though."

Jesus! I can't imagine a Khan/Alexander team up that can fail. "Who else does Alexander have on his side?" I ask.

"Cyrus II," he says. "Great guy. A little full of himself, but I like him."

The name sounds kind of familiar. Maybe it's from the Bible. I don't know.

"We also have Martin Luther down here. I'm not a fan, but he's got great organizational skill. Julius Caesar came on board, but it took a little sweet talking on Alexander's part. We've got a good lineup."

"What dogshit does Custer have?" my attorney asks.

"Henry VIII. Yeah, I know. It's not that surprising. He also has Hitler. He's an asshole, but he's a powerful asshole. He will be dealt with."

"This is the war to end all wars," I say. "I can't get my mind around the magnitude of this conflict. I can't grasp it."

"It's business as usual down here," Khan says. He gropes through his fur coat and comes up with some dark sticks of something and offers the handful to us. "Beef jerky?"

It's not everyday that Genghis Khan offers one beef jerky. I take it in an instant and stuff it in my mouth. It's tough but perfect. I wash it down with some Motherfucker and offer Khan a taste.

He takes it and swallows a healthy belt. "Thank you. That hit the spot." And hands the bottle back to me.

"So where's this battle?" my attorney asks. "Are they

all going to be there?"

"Yes. That phrase your friend used about this being the war to end all wars. People use that too often. There is always another giant fucking war looming in your near future. So it's big but not that big. Keep on this road. We'll get there eventually."

"You see?" my attorney asks me. "We're fucked. We shouldn't have picked him up."

"Forget that," I say. "We're on this road anyway. We would have gotten into the middle of it with or without him. Besides, with him on our side, maybe we can navigate the battle easier. He could be our ticket to getting through this thing in one piece."

"The rate we're going," Khan says, "we're not that far. If you have any defenses on this vehicle, you should raise them in about . . ." He rolls up his coat sleeve to reveal a Casio watch/calculator. "Two hours."

"We'll also need uppers," I say. I turn to look at Khan. "Do you have anything?"

He produces a jar. The label says that it's liquid phenyl cyclohexyl piperidine. PCP. Jesus. "Who do you think I am? I'm always prepared. You want some?"

"Maybe later," I say.

"I prefer to dip my cigarettes in this shit," Khan says. "But maybe we should just freebase this stuff. This shit will get you if you so much as dip your finger in it. Some side effects may include psychotic behavior, self-mutilation, invulnerability and cannibalism. That last one is my favorite."

I can all too easily see me gnawing on the bones of my enemies, so maybe we shouldn't do any PCP. I encourage legalizing all drugs, but PCP? That one always worries me.

We make idle conversation for the next hour, but when we start hearing the sounds of war—screams and roars and gunfire and explosions and crying—we start to get nervous. I'm tempted to smoke some weed to take the edge off, but that's too peaceful a drug. If we're going to be in the middle of a war zone soon, it would be better to have an angrier downer. I partake heavily of the Wild Turkey 101. Soon we can see smoke on the horizon. I can feel the Fear itching at me.

"I'm putting up the roof," my attorney says. "It's resistant to most weapons. So are the windows."

The roof encloses us, and we roll up the windows. It's stifling in here, so my attorney turns on the AC. He then hits another button, and machine guns raise out of our fenders. Yet another bumper transforms the front of the shark to a plow bent and sharpened in the middle. Spikes extend from the sides of the car. Something shifts in the back, but I can't see what that one does. We are a goddam war machine, and God's mercy on any swine who attempt to fuck with us.

"I think it's time for some uppers," my attorney says. "Khan, gimme one of those PCP cigs, would you?"

He grins and dips a cigarette in the liquid PCP. He hands it over and offers to me. "No thanks," I say. "I've got my own shit." I snort a couple of lines and crack a couple of amyls. Within seconds I feel like a war machine *without* the car.

Khan sticks a dropper into the liquid PCP and opens his mouth. One, two, three, four drops land on his tongue, and he presses it against the roof of his mouth. He takes some equipment out of his coat and starts piecing them together. Before long I realize that he's making an AK-47.

"Why not an M16?" I ask. "Maybe with a grenade launcher attached?"

"I like the Russians better," he says. "Easier to handle. It's like it's built for my hands. The M16 is too awkward. I'll leave that shit up to Caesar. He likes a good M16."

Fair enough. Who am I to question Genghis Khan's ability to slaughter people, anyway?

The sound of war is very loud now, and the smoke is

very close. We're getting ready to crest a hill, and I'm certain that when we do we'll be able to see the action for ourselves. Then with a little killing knowledge and a lot of luck, we'll get through this mess and be ready to face Nixon. Indeed.

In that moment I notice that there are no bats or manta rays here. They have rightly chosen to ignore this portion of Hell. Too bad we don't have this luxury.

We crest the hill, and sure enough we see the battle. Roman soldiers versus bluecoats versus cavemen versus Nazi soldiers versus Vietnam soldiers and so on. I've never seen anything like it, and I covered Vietnam fairly well. This is some kind of grim insanity. Under ordinary circumstances I wouldn't be able to get a grasp on this kind of thing, but I've got a head full of cocaine and amyls. I feel like a god.

"Let me out here," Genghis Khan says. "Thanks for the ride."

My attorney examines the situation. Already people are firing bullets and arrows and spears and even some rocks at us. "I can't do that. We're in the shit, man. We'll be killed if we open this door."

Khan doesn't give a fuck. With a roar he busts open my window and weasels his way out. He's very spry, and I can't help but feel sorry for anyone who tries to step in his path.

"How the fuck did he do that?!" my attorney screams.

"Never mind that!" I shout. "Keep driving!"

He stomps on the accelerator, and we zip forward, but before long we encounter a horse in the middle of the road. The man sitting on it wears a Confederate uniform. I'm from Louisville, so you can bet your goddam life that I know this man. He can only be JEB Stuart. The southern boy in me wants to shake his hand, but he's impeding our path. Just as I'm about to yell at him to get out of our way I see another familiar face to my right. He's in the midst of some kind of hand-to-hand battle, but

I'd recognize the swine anywhere. LBJ himself. He wears a red, white and blue bandana around his head and clutches a knife in his teeth. He's got two handguns, and he's firing into his enemy.

His gaze wanders over to me, and he freezes. I know he recognizes me. It's taking a moment to process this thought, but I know he's going to take a shot at me. I shoot him not because he's going to shoot me but on principle. It won't bring back the lives he needlessly sacrificed in Vietnam, but it makes me feel good to see the top of his skull sheared off, bandana and all.

There is an explosion that rocks the car. I turn to see someone has thrown a grenade at us. The windshield withstands the blow but it is darkened so badly that we can't see. I jam my thumb down on the button that fires the fender machine guns, and my attorney hits the wipers. When we can finally see again, JEB Stuart is gone, and there is a pile of bodies in front of us.

"Gear up!" I yell. "We'll never roll over those bodies unless we gear up!"

My attorney switches gears, and we thump and jump over the corpses. I keep my head low because without my window I'm exposed very badly. I don't relish taking another bullet in my head. My attorney seems unconcerned about this. His lips are drawn back, and his teeth are beared. I can hear him hissing through them.

I peek my head up just to make sure no one is drawing down on us. In that moment I see Audie Murphy gunning down a platoon of Nazis. I never really bought that movie about his life, but seeing him in action I'm awed. Maybe it really did happen. He certainly seems like a handy man to have around in a situation like this.

In a split second I see Genghis Khan. He is battling a mustached man who looks like Erich Ludendorff. Khan has no problem with the proto-Nazi. Ludendorff's head comes off like it was made of taffy, and Khan sticks his fingers in each eye socket. He rips to either side, and the head splits open like a piñata. And then he's off to fight someone else.

Bullets riddle the driver side of the shark, and my attorney hits a button which shoots the spikes out of his side of the car. They rain down on a group of Viet Cong, murdering them all. This is an absolute bloodbath. I desperately wish for it all to be over. Looking out the windshield does not give me much hope. We have miles to go before we're clear of this fight.

Something thumps down on top of the roof, and it moves around. Someone's up there, and it gives me the Fear. I poke my head out and see there's a ninja on top of us, and he has his katana blade out, ready to plunge it through the roof and into my attorney's head. I take aim with my .44 and blow him off the roof. I watch him flop down minus his head.

Then it comes over me. Holy shit! I just killed a ninja!

No time to bask in this victory. Something flies through the open window, and I see it's a hand grenade. My animal instinct takes over, and I fling it out of the car just in time. It explodes a few feet behind us. It rocks the shark, but we're fine. Nothing serious.

I see through the rear window a man who looks suspiciously like Captain Cook. What the hell is he doing here? He's a seaman, not a road warrior. What is going on? Never mind. Some redcoat just took him out. Odd. Weren't they on the same side? I guess it's a fitting end to a man who was killed by the very people who worshipped him.

"Shit!" my attorney screams. He whips the wheel to the right, and we're riding on the desert, shooting up clouds of smoke as our tires squeal. I look ahead of us and see a giant fucking tank. It's turning its barrel on us, but it can't move fast enough to keep up. However, if we get back on the road, it will have plenty of time to zero in on us.

My attorney's eyes are wide and his teeth are gritted as

he looks up into the rearview mirror. We're back on the road, and his finger is hovering over a button. When he judges we're in the right place, he slams his finger down. Something launches from the back of the car, and it goes right down the tank's cannon. I hear an explosion, and the barrel splinters. Smoke pours out of the tank's windows, and it stops moving.

"That was too close," my attorney says. "That thing could have taken us out."

"You did good," I said. "I think the bastards are burning to death."

My attorney laughs. "Good. Good!"

I peer through the windshield and see someone riding on a horse's back. He's a grizzled old man with an eye patch and the reigns clutched in his teeth. Two Walker Colts are clutched in his hands, and he's riding down on us. He looks a lot like John Wayne. Jesus shit! Is that Rooster Cogburn? Was he a real man? Or maybe this is the guy he was based on. My attorney gets ready to fire the fender machine guns at him.

Holy shit. I think it really is the Duke. Not the character he plays but the actor himself. There's no one I'd rather face off against in a fist fight, so I'm glad we have guns on our side.

It turns out that we don't need them. Genghis Khan leaps out of nowhere and beheads the Duke with one fell swoop. His body continues charging forward, unaware that he's lost his head, but he falls off the horse, and the horse loses interest in us. It wanders off the road.

I don't know if I really believe what I see, but I think Genghis Khan winks at us. Maybe. In some weird way he has gotten the revenge he has always sought.

By now it seems that the warriors have decided we're too dangerous to fuck with. Very few attacks come upon us. I feel safe enough to look out the window and watch as we drive.

We see Hitler bristling with so many arrows it looks

like he might be a porcupine. Dogs eat and fuck his corpse. The tide is shifting. Clearly Alexander is going to come up on top of this thing.

A while later we see Custer. He's knife fighting with a Roman. It might be Julius Caesar, but I don't know for sure. They circle each other, and then some World War II grunts nail Custer and bad. There is nothing recognizable left of him.

We're nearly through the battle when we see Caligula holding aloft William Calley's head. I think Caligula gets a bad rap. Most of the sources we have of his lunacy weren't there at the time. The very few contemporaneous sources we have of him were written by his enemies. Maybe he was perfectly reasonable in his day. Who knows for sure? But the fact that he just killed Calley speaks volumes for the opposing side.

Whoops. Never mind. Caligula's fucking Calley's eye socket.

Finally we reach a point where the fight is thinning. Fewer people are around us. Fewer bullets and arrows fill the skies. Even the bats have returned. Maybe we're going to make it through this after all.

The world around us is quiet. There isn't a soul on this road. My attorney grins, and I can see his nose is bleeding over his teeth. I don't know how this happened, but it doesn't matter. *We made it.*

"That's what I call driving," he says. "I need something to calm down. Where's the hash?"

I pack a pipe and hand it over with a lighter. For myself I down several healthy gulps of Wild Turkey. We're almost out. Dammit.

We're both feeling much more comfortable. My attorney says that within ten minutes we'll be at the ninth circle, free from the madness behind us.

Exactly ten more minutes, at the very edge of the eighth circle, we come upon a Native American sitting in the road, cross-legged, contemplating. My attorney goes to fire the fender machine guns, but I stay his hand. "Stop," I tell him.

"Why? We don't have time for this."

"He's not bothering us. I want to see what he's doing. Maybe get a recording."

My attorney grumbles, but he pulls the car over. I get out and approach the man. He looks very familiar. "Greetings," I say. "What are you doing here? You're going to be hit by a car if you're not careful. Hell, my attorney wanted to shoot you dead. Luckily he's under my control. Most of the time. Do you need help?"

He turns the saddest pair of eyes up to me, and we lock our gaze. Tears stream down his cheeks and pour off the ledge of his jaw. "I am tired," he says. "My heart is sick and sad. From where the sun now stands, I will fight no more forever."

Something burns in my eyes. He's right. I am tired, especially after everything we've just been through. I rub at my face, and my hands come away wet. "Do you need a lift?" I ask. My throat feels almost too tight to speak.

"No," he says. "This is my damnation. I will never move from this spot. But thank you for the offer."

"Chief Joseph," I say.

He offers a smile, but his eyes do not light up. "Someone remembers. I'm glad."

"Goodbye," I say. "Don't take any guff from these fucking swine."

He nods, and I get back in the car. My attorney looks at me, eyebrows raised.

"Do you want me to smear him all over this road?" he asks.

"No," I say. "Drive around him. Leave him alone."

My attorney wants to question me further, but he doesn't. He is paid by the hour. We drive around Chief Joseph and into the ninth circle. We're almost there, Nixon. Tuck your dick back and prepare for the worst.

8

*Time to come down. Relaxation in Hell. Treacherous
swine. Welcome to the No Fun Club. The end of the line.
It's all or nothing. Hell's DEA agent.*

We ride in silence for maybe twenty minutes. My
attorney looks like a statue. I don't even know if he's all
there. He's still wearing his sunglasses, but I'm pretty
sure he's got a thousand yard stare. The battle has scarred
us in ways we could never explain, much less understand.

My blood is still pumping. I think it's time to come
down. I get into the hash, and I offer some to my attorney.
He shakes his head. "I'm already crashing."

"Maybe we should get to a hotel," I say. "It's been a
rough day. We've pushed this thing as far as we can. We
should probably get our shit together."

"We can't get a hotel around here. Hell, we can't buy
anything while we're on this circle."

"Why not? We have plenty of teeth to barter."

"Everyone here is a treacherous swine. That's what this
circle is for. Dante was right about that much. This is the
No Fun Club."

"Well shit," I say. I hoist my .44 and wave it around.
"Guns. We have them. We can stop anyone from fucking
with us with hardware like this. We'll hold them down
and gang fuck them."

"If we stay in a hotel, I guarantee we'll wake up with
our throats slit and our teeth bashed out. It's better to just
pull over and get some sleep. Maybe get into the heroin.
My shoulder's killing me."

The landscape has gone from desert to a more rocky
area. There isn't a lot of shade, but there is plenty of
room to see someone sneaking up on us. "That's a good
idea," I say. "We'll sleep in shifts. I'm still kind of wired.
You sleep first. I'll keep us safe."

"Are you sure you can handle it?" he asks. "This is no joke. There are savages out here."

"Relax," I say. "We have to get our strength up for Nixon. We're almost there, aren't we?"

He peers off into the horizon, his tongue running over his teeth. "Yeah. I can almost smell him. He stinks of melted pennies."

That makes sense. He pulls over and heads off-road so far that we can no longer see it. Only then is he content to turn off the ignition. Not before putting the roof up, though. "Can't be too careful," he says.

I glance at my broken out window. Indeed.

My attorney gets into the drug kit and finds the shit he bought off of Lincoln. The works look a bit too dingy for my likes, but my attorney doesn't seem to mind. He cooks up what seems like a dangerous dose to me, but I think he can take it. When it's ready in a needle, he ties himself off and injects the inside of his elbow like a pro. Wow. The drug has gotten a hold of him pretty quickly. How long ago had he been squeamish about needles? How long, indeed?

Bliss soothes out his face, and he drops into a quick slumber. His eyes are moving beneath their lids, and a slow smile creeps across his face. He slumps down behind the wheel, and he almost looks like a sleeping newborn baby.

The hours pass, and I watch as the bats and manta rays return to the sky. They're more at home here, away from the horrible battle miles behind us. They no longer scare me. It's kind of hypnotic, and it brings peace to my heart. I could almost sleep to something like this. But not now. I keep a careful watch on the world around us.

Nothing disturbs us. When my attorney comes out of it, he cooks up just a little bit more. "To keep me level," he says. "Don't worry. It won't be enough to make me pass out. As your attorney I advise that you do some of this shit. It will relax you."

What the hell? Why not? We're almost at the end of the line. What can it hurt?

He does himself first, and then I start cooking up my own shot. It takes a bit of trouble to get the needle in the right place, but when I nail it home and push the plunger, I feel such great relief that I don't even bother to take the needle out of my arm. My attorney does this and packs it away.

I don't pass out, but I feel incredibly mellow. The drug fills my head and lungs with cotton candy. Soothing cotton candy. I peer at the world through half-closed eyelids. It flashes by, and I don't give a single solitary fuck about what I see.

It's beautiful.

More time than I think passes. There are hitchhikers everywhere on this road. They all look fucking crazy. More than once my attorney has to shoot them in the head. He doesn't pull over to get the teeth, though. This place is too dangerous for that kind of thing. Not that it matters. Our journey is almost over. Nixon is almost in our hands.

I doze for a while, and when I wake up I feel too groggy. I get one of the amyls under my nose, and that wakes me the fuck up. I'm alert, and my head is darting back and forth.

"Finally," my attorney says. "I thought you'd never wake up. I was getting ready to dump your carcass out the side."

"You'd never do that," I say. "You need me."

"You're worthless to me dead. You should never have taken that heroin."

Maybe. Shit. "Are we almost there?"

"It'll be an hour before we reach the center of Hell," he says. "Reserve the uppers. We'll need them soon."

He's my attorney, so I get into the hash and whiskey. The Turkey is almost gone. Why not finish it up? Soon it won't matter. We'll be in a one-on-one fight with Nixon.

No matter how that ends, we won't need our drug collection anymore.

"What happens when we kill Nixon?" I ask.

"I don't know. Maybe we become the new rulers of Hell. That would be groovy."

Maybe we *become* Nixon. Jesus, what a terrible thought! I inhale a lungful of hash, hold it in, take down two shots worth of Wild Turkey and blow out the smoke. Yes. This is the place to be. There is no finer place in the world—or the afterlife—than right here, in this frame of mind. Maybe another dose of heroin would hit the spot.

No. I can't do that. That isn't a trip for the likes of me.

Forty-five minutes later my attorney pulls over. "This is it, man. The point of no return. Toss the downers in the back seat. We want all of the uppers. Now."

There isn't much cocaine left, but we carefully divide what remains of the brick. We also divvy up the crank pills and the amyls. My attorney starts ingesting all of his cut.

"Jesus. Do you think that's a good idea?"

My attorney turns his eyes on me, and they're on fire with bad craziness. "We're closing in on the end, man. There is no other option. It's all or nothing." His cocaine is already gone, and he's chasing down the crank with some Motherfucker.

I find this unacceptable. We don't know what trickery Nixon has in store for us. I do about half of my cocaine, and I take half of the crank with some Motherfucker. My share of the amyls don't amount to much, so I only break one of them under my nose. The other two, along with the rest of my share of uppers, goes into my pocket. I hope my attorney doesn't notice.

He bunches up like a clenched fist. "Let's do this!"

I roar to the heavens. My battle cry must be heard all the way back to the gates of Hell.

My attorney jams his fat foot onto the accelerator, and we zip into the future.

Five minutes later we see it. There is a gate ahead, and it reaches all the way up the sky. There is no top. The door is not that big, though; it's just tall enough to let a ten-foot motherfucker in, wide enough for us to drive the shark through. Electricity crackles along the length of this wall, and there is barbed wire all over it. No one is meant to cross, but we will. I check my gun. I have enough ammo for what's in it and one more full cylinder. That's fine. If I run out, I still have the Extractor.

"How much ammo do you have?" I ask.

My attorney, one hand on the wheel, the other on his weapon, checks. "I have one full load. After that, I just have the Gerber. But that shouldn't be a problem. Nixon will be dead long before I run out."

I don't like the odds. It can't just be as simple as driving through the gate and assassinating Nixon. He's a tricky bastard. I don't trust him or this job. We have to have a contingency plan. I am suddenly grateful for holding on to half of my drugs.

Suddenly I feel the need for one of the hunks of Carcosa. I don't know why, but I grab one of them and slip it into my pocket, the one that doesn't have the rest of my drugs. They shouldn't mix.

"You're not going to need that," my attorney says.

"It's for our celebration," I say. "For later."

I can tell he doesn't buy it, but he doesn't object. He keeps driving, speeding toward the final gate between us and our prey.

We make the final approach, and my attorney stops the car in front of the gate. He lays into the horn, and it can be heard for miles. It plays the Jimi Hendrix version of "The Star Spangled Banner." It swells my heart. For as much bullshit as our government causes, I can't help but be a staunch patriot. Without the United States, a freak like me would not be allowed to live. I'd have been smothered at birth anywhere else, or maybe thrown off a cliff. Take it back to ancient times, and they would have put me in a basket and thrown me in the river. Dark times, indeed.

"What now?" I ask.

"We wait for them to open the door," my attorney says.

"They probably know us. They'd never let us in."

"They have to. It's Hell Code."

Hell Code? This is the first he's mentioned of this. I wonder what else is a part of the Hell Code. I'm about to ask when the gate clicks and slowly creaks open. My attorney doesn't even check to make sure it's safe. He drives fearlessly through, and his hand wanders down to the .357. This is a good idea, so I clutch my .44 tightly, ready for action.

We're in what I can only describe as the foyer to a mansion, or maybe a castle. There is no ceiling, or it's too tall for me to see. A sense of unease settles in the pit of my gut, and I keep turning my head, looking for any threat to us.

"There!" my attorney says. He points through the windshield.

A shadowy form emerges. It looks human, but there is too much mass near the head. I can't see much except for a slight glitter effect. And then it comes out into the light, and it's a vision I never expected to see. I can't even breathe, it's so shocking.

My attorney gets out of the car and approaches the figure, gun in his hand. I don't know if I should follow him, but I get out of the car, also with my gun dangling by my side. My attorney stops just outside of arm's reach from the man.

"I never thought it would be you," he says.

"It makes sense to me, brother," the man says.

"I saw the picture. I couldn't believe a barbiturate freak like you would be by Nixon's side. It had to be some kind of trick."

"I walked into the White House with a loaded gun," the man says. "I gave it to Nixon as a present. Uh-huh. I love that man, and I'd give my life to protect him."

My attorney spat. "Elvis fucking Presley. I used to like you. I thought you were all right for a honky."

Yes. Dear God! It *is* Elvis Presley, but he's got three heads. Right now he talks out of the center one, but the others are sneering at us. One of them barks like a dog.

"I can't let you boys through," Elvis says. "As your celebrated American icon, I advise that you turn back and go to the circles you deserve. Otherwise . . ." He strikes some kind of kung fu pose, his hands extended like shovel blades. "Otherwise, I'm going to have to use my karate on you."

My attorney whips up his gun and fires, almost point blank, into Elvis's center head. The King flies back, and I think that's that. There's no coming back from a gunshot wound like that. Then Elvis comes up in a crouch. His lips spread wide open. Holy shit! He has the bullet in his teeth! That's impossible! But no, this is Hell. A lot of impossible things are very possible down here.

He laughs through the bullet, and I know we don't have much time. I take careful aim at his heart and pull the trigger. Twice. There's no way he can avoid these bullets.

His hand flashes by in a blur. He falls back, but he comes up pretty quickly. There are my bullets, caught between the fingers of that hand. Shit. Our guns are useless against this animal. We'll have to do something else.

My attorney realizes this at the same time. He holsters the gun and pulls out his Gerber Mini-Magnum. He flashes his grin. "I can play without the guns."

Elvis holds out his hand flat, palm up. He curls his fingers. "Bring it," his left head says.

My attorney moves, and Elvis's center head spits out the bullet at a velocity quicker than even the .357 can fire. It catches my attorney in the belly, blowing out his guts behind him. I can see the exit wound, and it's about the size of a dish. It doesn't stop him, though. Madly, he surges forward, the Gerber flashing.

Elvis doesn't seem to notice. He flings my bullets back at me, but I'm quick enough to duck down behind the shark. One bullet zings off the hood, but the other punches through and nearly gets me. I peek my head up, and I see the King has locked my attorney's arm behind him and is pushing up. Either my attorney will drop the knife, or he'll get his arm broken. Probably both. Only one of Elvis's heads is looking at me. Maybe I can nail him.

I take a shot, but not at anywhere vital. I just want to hurt him this time. I act like I'm about to shoot for his head, but then I dart my gun down and take a shot at his foot. His right hand zips down, but he's not fast enough. Success! His foot explodes into hunks of meat. Elvis howls, and he lets go of my attorney. As I take a shot at Elvis's right head, my attorney plunges the Gerber into the King's leg and jerks it down, ripping off his kneecap. Elvis catches my bullet in his teeth, but when my attorney destroys his leg, Elvis starts choking on the bullet. One of his hands goes to his throat, and I can see the other two heads can feel it, too. They may have three heads, but they all share the same throat.

Elvis may be in trouble, but he's not down and out yet. He karate chops my attorney's neck, and he falls. Not too far, though. He still has more drugs in his system than is possible to have in real life. He rises like the devil and tries to cut out Elvis's guts. Elvis blocks the attempt and turns the knife in my attorney's hand so it looks like he's about to stab himself.

I shoot again, this time at Elvis's healthy kneecap, and it explodes so badly that his leg bends backwards. With a scream, Elvis falls, and my attorney follows, one of his hands on the King's throat, his other hand still struggling with the knife. Elvis's free hand seeks my attorney's face, and I see he's trying to put a thumb in my attorney's eye.

I have two bullets left. I'd better make them count. I draw down on one of Elvis's heads, but my attorney is in the way. I can't get a clear shot. Elvis shoves his thumb down, and my attorney screams. I can see that he no longer has that eye, but the drugs are pushing him forward. He's almost got the knife turned around, but I don't think he's going to make it.

Fuck it. My attorney would want me to take the shot. I drop the hammer, and one of Elvis's heads loses its top. The pompadour flies right off of his brain and splats against the wall. It sticks there for a moment before it slides down on a greasy smear of blood.

The other heads sense the danger, and they push my attorney away. Elvis tries to stand, but with his legs fucked up like that, he can barely crawl forward. Yet he's still trying to get me, and I know all of his attention is taken up. There's no way I can sneak another gunshot at him. I take aim, though, because I'm not going down without a fight.

My attorney leaps like a gorilla onto Elvis's back and jams his .357 against the back of Elvis's left head. He fires two shots into it, completely disintegrating it, leaving only the center head.

The center head, still choking on the bullet stuck in his throat, is trying to form words. My attorney yanks on him, turning him over. He jams his knee onto Elvis's chest, and the bullet pops out. Now my attorney has his . 357 stuffed into Elvis's mouth.

"A little less conversation," my attorney says, "a little more action." And he empties his gun into Elvis's last remaining head. The King lets out a tremendous fart, and his arms and legs flail for a moment, but soon he is still and dead.

I see the brown stain, and I realize that maybe it wasn't just a fart. I don't think any less of the man. He died on the toilet, after all, like any good American icon.

"We got the bastard," my attorney says. His remaining

eye rolls wildly in its socket, and he's grinning like a madman. "This is why the war on drugs will always be won by drugs. They work. They helped us kill Hell's DEA agent."

Indeed.

We hear a clapping sound, and our heads whip around to see . . . dear God! It really is the end! Nixon has just entered the room, and he's grinning at us, clapping his hands as if he's pleased with our work.

I glance at my attorney. "It's all come to this."

He nods his head. "Let's get him."

We advance on Nixon, murder in our eyes and drugs on our side.

9

The end of the line.

"That's far enough." Nixon holds a hand up, and some primitive part of our brains kicks in. We both stop. This grim specter has an odd gleam in his shit-mist eyes, and he wears a grin that shows no teeth. He looks taller than I remember. Maybe his time in Hell has made him a bigger man. He's not wearing elevator shoes. Maybe he's stuffing his heels. Hm.

"There's no escaping this, you swine," I say. "This is the end of the line. For good or ill. We will destroy you, but we won't eat you. Not even the dogs will gnaw your bones. They have taste."

Nixon chuckles. "You might have been good back in your day. Hell, you gave me a run for my money. But you lost steam. No one gave a shit about you until you blew your brains out. Then, out of the blue, you were the Patron Saint of Journalism. You're a joke. You always have been. Right, Uncle Duke?"

Shit. That one does nail me. It still gets to me whenever someone recognizes me from *Doonesbury*. I'll have to skin Nixon alive to make me feel better. But I know his tactic, and I hold back. He wants me to surge forward. I don't know why, but I know enough to keep myself in check.

Nixon knows it, too. He turns his gaze on my attorney. "Ah. And your Samoan sidekick. I should have known you'd follow your white master everywhere he went."

"You bastard!" my attorney roars. The Gerber Mini-Magnum is suddenly in his hands, and he lurches toward Nixon, riding the last of the drugs in his system on a mission to take out the former president.

Nixon folds his arms in a smug manner, and death rays shoot out of his eyes. He nods his head, and my attorney's knife arm comes off like it was never attached. Nixon shakes his head, and my attorney crumples to the floor without his legs. He gibbers like a madman, and much to my shock, his remaining arm tries to drag him closer to Nixon. He's just not strong enough, though. Lucky for him, the death rays cauterized his wounds. He might yet die of shock, but he won't die from blood loss. Maybe I can put him back together like some mad, Brown Buffalo Humpty Dumpty.

"I love to see a man squirm," Nixon says. "Gets my dick hard." He points to his crotch, and there is a noticeable bulge there.

My attorney screams, and it isn't just from the pain. I recognize the helpless sound of his inner turmoil. Jesus. Nixon has death rays coming from his eyes! How can we fight something like that?

"You want to help him," Nixon says.

I nod. "He's a good man. I think I can help him."

"I promise not to hurt you," Nixon says. "Go to his aid. It's worthless, anyway."

Nixon is not a man to be trusted. I don't know how I can defend himself if this turns out to be a lie. Still, I go to my man and kneel next to him. He whispers something to me, but I can't hear it.

"What are you saying?" I ask. I dip my head closer to my attorney's mouth.

"The button," he whispers. "Sit in the driver seat and hit the button. If you have any uppers left, as your attorney I recommend you take them."

"What does the button do?" I ask. I keep my voice low so Nixon doesn't hear.

"You'll know when the time is right." My attorney's eyes are filled with blood tears. "Get the bastard for me, man. I want to die knowing that you took him the fuck out."

"Agreed," I say. "No mercy for this swine."

An explosion from behind. I whip around, ready for anything. I see that while I was occupied with my attorney, Nixon stole the reel-to-reel recorder from the shark. He had just thrown it into the air and shot it down with his death rays. Rage flows through me. There goes my story. My evidence. Everything I have encountered on this savage journey into the heart of Hell. Gone.

"Are you done yet?" Nixon asks. He looks bored.

I stand up and turn my head until my neck cracks. Nixon looks too smug for my likes. There is nothing I can do against him. I hate to admit defeat, but I'm not too stupid to turn this into a Butch and Sundance situation. I have to outthink the bastard. I used to be good at this kind of thing. Have the drugs addled my brain too much? Have I really gone over the edge?

Time to find out.

"Look," I say, "you're right. You're too powerful down here. I'm not going to fuck with you, Nixon. Not anymore. You're too good for this game. I'm just going to get back into my car and drive away. Is that OK with you?"

He nods, but he doesn't say anything. I back away from my attorney and slip into the driver seat of the shark. The key is still in the ignition, but I don't go for that. I start rifling through my pockets, and Nixon doesn't like that. His hands are now at his sides, and he's alert.

I take out the drugs. "Don't worry. It's for the road. I came a long way, so I'll need a good dose to get me back on the path."

"Very well," Nixon says. "Be quick about it."

I snort the rest of my cocaine. There's a lot of it, but I make sure to get it all down. I pop the rest of the crank with some Motherfucker, and my heart is racing like crazy.

It's the amyls that put me over the top. I crack them all at once and breathe them all down. I am God. I'm bigger than any motherfucker in Hell and beyond. My dick alone is bigger than the shit-hammer of truth. There is nothing that can stop me. Nothing.

I jam my thumb down on the button my attorney never explained to me. I feel the car shifting around me. It cradles me as it folds in on itself. I'm so fucked up I don't know what it's doing, but by the end I know what has happened. The shark has turned into a humanoid robot, and it has machine guns for fists. The robotic face has eye lasers. Its nipples can shoot grenades.

Nixon stares at me, agape. I think I finally have the bastard on the ropes. There's no avoiding this now. It's time to end this fucker once and for all.

And then Nixon surprises me. He snaps his finger, and pieces of metal fly out of nowhere, encasing his body until only his face is visible through a sheet of what is undoubtedly bulletproof glass. Jesus! He's become a giant robot. Maybe a bit bigger than mine, but I know I can take him.

"Do your worst!" Nixon screams. His breath fogs up the glass.

I roar and let loose with the machine guns. Bullets spark off Nixon's mech, but nothing seems to be having an effect. Before I can try the grenades, Nixon plunges forward with his death ray eyes. They rock my robot, but it's not damaged at all. I have to regain my footing, and soon I launch grenades. Nixon manages to dodge them, and they explode somewhere in the darkness behind him.

Now he fires bullets at me, and they have the exact same effect as mine did on him. Nothing but some pretty ricochets. He quickly gives up on those and tries the death rays again. By now I have a better grip on the controls, and I roll out of his way. I'm now at his feet, and I wrap both robot arms around his ankles, yanking him down to the floor. He tries to push my robot head down, but I'm a sudden bastard. I get around his wavering arms and grasp at his robot throat. He peels my fingers away, but that's what I expect. With my other hand, I clutch at his robot eyes, and I manage to tear one of them out. It explodes, and I see that it's taken out my robot hand. Not that it matters. I have him in my grasp.

Whoops! Maybe not. He drives both arms up between us and pushes me aside. I'm on my back, and I don't know how to straighten this fucking thing. It takes some maneuvering, but just as I get the hang of it I see Nixon looming over me. The bastard is grinning like a hyena. He's turning his remaining death ray on me, but I lash out with my foot, knocking him down so badly that he's on top of me. I didn't expect that, but we're practically in missionary position with him as the top. We're face to face, and the only thing separating us is the translucent window over his head. He's so mad with joy he's licking the glass like some freak at a peep show.

Fuck him. I still have my .44. I whip it out and press it against the bulletproof glass. Even though I can't hear him, he laughs. I empty the goddam gun into that glass. Each bullet leaves its mark and fogs up the surface, but they don't do much damage.

Except that last one. The glass cracks. Nixon looks nervous, but I'm out of ammo. There's nothing I can do. Not even a well placed punch will break through.

Good thing I still have the Extractor. I give the glass one good lick with the blackjack, and it shatters. Now there is nothing separating me from Nixon. I rear back to slug him with the Extractor, but he throws a *shuriken*—where the hell did he get that?!—at me. It only grazes my hand, but it's enough to get me to drop the Extractor. Shit. Maybe I can still beat the fuck out of him with my bare hands, but will that be enough?

The robots struggle against each other, and Nixon has the shark in a bear hug, bringing us so close that we can kiss each other if we had a mind for that kind of thing. I can smell his rotten breath, and he laughs in my face.

"It's over! Outlaw journalism is a thing of the past! You're a relic! You'll be forgotten as soon as all of your friends die! How does it feel to be doomed?"

Then I remember something. Sure, Nixon was a heavy drinker in his time. I'll talk shit about him from dusk till dawn, but I will always give that to him. He can out-drink the best of them and walk out as straight as a soldier.

But that doesn't mean he can withstand a hunk of Carcosa. I yank the crumpled lump from my pocket and jam it into his laughing face. With my other hand I clamp down on his jaw. He struggles against me, but there's nothing he can do. The shit has already contacted his tongue. There's no way out of this trip.

His robot scores a lucky shot on mine, and the shark's head is suddenly a useless hump of metal. The robot shrieks, and it can no longer stand. It's transforming back into a car. I can no longer keep the Carcosa in Nixon's mouth. He spits it out like a wad of gum and falls back. His robot is only as good as him, and whether he likes it or not, he's got a head full of Carcosa. He'll be a gibbering wreck before long.

"What did you do to me?!" he screams.

The shark is damaged but not so badly that it can't be driven. I get out of the driver seat and approach the flailing wreck of Nixon's robot. "Nothing," I say to him. "You're about to go on a trip. You're doomed, you bastard. To quote a pigfucker, 'Fuck the doomed.'"

He closes his eyes, writhing in mental agony, but he doesn't know that it won't protect him from the horrors about to descend on him. No. Nothing can, and I don't feel the slightest bit of remorse. He is doomed. Fuck the doomed. Right. Throw his words right back at him.

Nixon. You should have been a freak like the rest of us. If you were, you wouldn't be in this position now.

I rush to my attorney. He is still alive, and his eyes are rolling wildly. "Did you get him?" he asks. His voice is a pitiful imitation of what it once was.

"He's on a trip he'll never come back from," I say.

"Good. *Good.* Stomp on his balls for me."

"You got it," I say. "Is there anything I can do for you?"

"The heroin," he whispers. "Give me the rest of the heroin."

Normally I would advise against such a thing. One talks of a heroic dose when it comes to mushrooms. Applied to this amount of heroin, it would kill even Keith Richards. But my attorney hasn't got much living left in him. Why not send him off on a wave of euphoria?

As Nixon's robot still thrashes in the midst of lunacy, I go back to the shark, to our drug kit, and I cook up the ultimate heroin shot. There's no coming back from something like this. It's kind of beautiful. I tie him off and shoot him up. Instant satisfaction comes across his face.

"Thank you, man. You're the best client I've ever had."

"And you're a hell of an attorney," I say. "When God made you, he broke the mold."

"I liked our Vegas trip," he says. "It was the most fun I've ever had. Things got ugly every once in a while, but we did good work there. God's work."

"Indeed," I say.

He holds up his hand, and I clasp it. In this moment, we are warriors, and we have destroyed all of our enemies. We've walked a road of bones, and we stomped the terra, and we killed like champions. I've never felt closer to a man than in this moment.

And then he dies with a grin on his face.

I release his hand and place it over his heart. I close his remaining eye. Then I stand and go back to the car for more drugs. My heart is still kicking the shit out of the rest of my guts, and I need to come down. The last of the hash should do the trick. As I load up my pipe I see the dog. I'd completely forgotten about it. Maybe now was the perfect time to use it.

I grab Checkers by the collar and walk back to Nixon's robot. It's moving so fast that it's malfunctioning. Soon all he has left is his right arm, and all it does is twitch. Nixon's eyes are rolling in their sockets, and he's hyperventilating. If only Kissinger can see him now.

"Hey Nixon," I say. "I found Checkers"

I hold the dead dog before me like a talisman, and Nixon screams so hard he ruptures his throat. Blood oozes from the corners of his mouth. I don't know what his Carcosa-soaked mind is imagining, but it's not good, not for Nixon. Drool mixes with the blood, and it's spraying all over the place. I think he's having a seizure.

I throw the dead dog at him, and he nearly jumps out of his skin. He coughs blood all over his beloved Checkers, and he jerks so swiftly he looks like a marionette being played by a man who doesn't know what he's doing.

I've had my fun. I have the advantage, and you can never predict Carcosa. For all I know, Nixon will ride this out and come out on top. I can't have that. My bullets are all gone, and I can't find the Extractor. Luckily the Gerber hasn't gone far from my attorney's severed arm. I pick it up and head back to Nixon. His eyes are blank, and he's gibbering about nothing. Nothing makes sense.

Cutting off a man's head takes time and determination. I don't know how the ancient savages did it, but I manage it in about five minutes. Getting through the spine is the hardest part, but there is nothing more satisfying in the world than cutting off your greatest enemy's head and holding it out to the world by its hair. I roar like an ape, and I spike his head on the floor. It bursts like a melon.

Finally, out of breath, I collapse. I've never felt so drained than I do now. I guess I'm the new ruler of Hell.

I look out the gate and see that Hell's denizens have gathered, and they're cheering my name. I see Genghis Khan among them, and he's wearing a blood stained grin. The air stinks of death and burned gasoline.

No. I can't be the ruler of Hell. Not even the biggest king-hell bastard would allow something like that, and I don't think I would like the gig. I can't be the leader. I'm an outlaw. Outlaws aren't supposed to be in the system.

There are no more bullets. The only drugs that can kill me are gone. There's the Carcosa, but I don't know if that will do the job. The Gerber isn't long enough for a good dose of *seppuku*. Jesus, what's left to me?

I scramble through the trunk, looking for anything that can do the job. I'm about to give up when I find a stray bullet for the .44. Yes, when you carry that much firepower and that much ammo, something is liable to slip through the cracks. Good.

I load up the gun and shove the barrel into my mouth. I take a look at my attorney who grins even in death. I look at Nixon's remains, and I can't help but smile. My job is done here.

I don't think about it. I just pull the trigger.

Nothing happens. Shit. Maybe Satan can't kill himself.

Then I remember what my attorney said about never dying in Hell. I look at his remains and shudder to think of how he'll feel when that heroin wears off.

I turn away from his mangled body to look out through the gate, and the denizens of Hell are already gathering. They know their bastard ruler is no more, and they've come to gaze upon the new king. They chant my name over and over. They cheer their new king. They have been saved from the greatest monster they've ever known.

I'm the king. Long live me.

Jesus. Can the poor bastards grasp that?!

Dedicated to the memory of my hero, Hunter S. Thompson. I hope I did right by you. If there's an afterlife, the Wild Turkey is on me.

-- John Bruni

John Bruni is the author of *Tales of Questionable Taste* and *Poor Bastards and Rich Fucks*, both from StrangeHouse Books, *Dong of Frankenstein* for New Kink and *Strip*, a crime novel from the now defunct Musa, but it has been rereleased through Riot Forge. His shorter work has appeared in many places, most notably *Shroud, Hardboiled, Morpheus Tales, Cthulhu Sex Magazine, Tales of the Talisman* and a number of anthologies, including *Triple Zombie* from Spanking Pulp Press, *A Hacked-Up Holiday Massacre* from Pill Hill Press and the critically acclaimed *Vile Things* from Comet Press. He edited *Strange Sex 3* for New Kink. He was the poetry editor of *MiddleWestern Voice*, and he was the editor and publisher of *Tabard Inn*, a fiction magazine. He lives in Elmhurst, IL, which is definitely not bat country.

AUTHOR'S NOTE

I came to Hunter S. Thompson fairly late in life. It was Terry Gilliam's brilliant movie based on *Fear and Loathing in Las Vegas* that did it for me. I saw it in college in the theater. I tracked down the book and experienced its splendors for myself. As soon as I gobbled it up I had to have more. In no time flat I had his entire library (even the difficult to find *Curse of Lono*), and I had all of his howling and raving in my head. I bought every new book by HST the very day it was released. It was a very sad day when I turned on my radio and heard that he'd shot himself at his Owl Creek compound.

I prepared for writing this novella in a number of ways. I don't ordinarily ingest substances while creating. Sometimes when I edit since it makes me feel like it's someone else's work, and I can really cut loose then. But very rarely during the actual writing itself. I changed that rule for this one. I would start with a few belts of Wild Irish Rose, which is a very good booster, kind of like putting a blasting cap on dynamite. I would then read from the graphic novel adaptation, which essentially tells its story with direct quotes from the book. While doing so, I would graduate to Wild Turkey 101, and that's when Doc's voice really started to permeate my mind. I started thinking in his speech pattern. Then I would go downstairs to my computer, where I kept my copy of *Fear and Loathing in Las Vegas*. I would open the book up at random and drop my finger in. Wherever it landed, I read for at least a page. As I got closer to the end I might have ingested, uh, other substances. Maybe. And then I was ready to let Doc take over. I think I killed like a champion. Let me know what you think.

-- *John Bruni*

JOHN BRUNI
WRITER OF FUCKED UP SHIT

WWW.TALESOFQUESTIONABLETASTE.COM
WWW.TALESOFUNSPEAKABLETASTE.BLOGSPOT.COM
WWW.FORCEDVIEWING.COM
WWW.FACEBOOK.COM/JOHN.BRUNI.775
WWW.FACEBOOK.COM/TALESOFQUESTIONABLETASTE
WWW.AMAZON.COM/AUTHOR/JOHNBRUNI
@TUSITALABRUNI ON TWITTER

DR. HILL

It was near sunset on some lonely stretch of asphalt in the middle of God's nowhere before I questioned my conscience. I remember turning to look at the man I'd come to know as Jiminy and wondered as to his motives. We had been heading in this direction now for a solid hour. The last place we had stopped was some forbidden roadhouse that even the dust-dwelling locals seemed to give a wide birth. Its walls were the colour of urine stained sheets with dead flies blotting the windows that overlooked the road. A happy-dirty little boy of around maybe 5 years, sporting a maniacal grin which spoke to

103

us of his future employment as an axe-wielding psychopath sat on a wooden chair by the door. Jiminy had asked the greasy waitress for directions. All I remembered is she had pointed in the direction of the horizon and made mention that if we came to the skeleton of a dead camel chances were we had blown severely off course. Jiminy at this juncture thought it best to clear his mind to absorb all of this new information. He cut a loud fart, which didn't seem to bother the waitress. By the look of her she had seen greater horrors in this deserted hell.

The psycho kid by the door had left his seat and had taken it upon himself to follow along behind as I carefully took stock of the four aisles of products on offer. There was the usual brake fluid, shaving cream and condoms. This is the best these poor wretches have to offer I remember thinking to myself. I could imagine the grotesque late night orgies that the waitress, who generously was giving us the time of day, would put on for whatever man, brave enough, was found stumbling in her bed chamber. Had such an event produced the young child that now followed me? I thought it definitely possible, if not likely. There were three glass doors to the rear of the space that kept the cold beverages safe from the hot wind that was slowly eating everything else. I procured my friend and myself two six-packs of Funky Munky, some ridiculously overpriced boutique beer that was fixed with a rather elaborate label depicting said Funky Munky drowning his sorrows with the very product he was peddling. This everlasting Munky; the hallucinatory properties of the image were mind-blowing. The fear crept over me as I realised that the Munky on the label had the same label on the beer he was greedily partaking of. Damn him, was my inner monologue's cry to heaven.

I rounded out my purchases with a quart of rum. This mixed with the beer would soothe us should we reach the end of the black road and find a sign on the rusty gate there saying, 'back in 5 mins.' Jiminy was making no headway with the wilting flower of womanhood behind the elaborately contrived and colourful display of bubble gum. If he thought he was going to get lucky and become the father of the brother of the tiny demon that I knew was lurking somewhere behind me in the dusty, roach-grave corners of this fine establishment then he was one of the more deceived.

We paid for the drinks and hit the road.

"She was a fine girl," said Jiminy, a full three Munkys into the dialogue.

"You my friend are a character of poor choices. That woman would fuck you then eat you alive. That or she'd cut you up and feed you to her young."

"She was a fine girl indeed," he said again.

Was he trying to convince me, was this some kind of strange mantra he was concocting to justify sex with a mutant of the wastelands? I pondered this a moment and then drank more. The cold Munky in my hand was doing its work. Soon I would forget all about that desolate place and its frail inhabitants. After all, we were on our way to a festive event of a magnitude neither of us could comprehend; that was, at least until we manage to tighten our grip, open the drunken nirvana's equivalent of Pandora's Box and take a peek inside.

Jiminy saw the broken-down Chevy long before I did. The strange character that leaned against the hood while copious amounts of steam poured out from the grill was a magnificent specimen of madness and poise. Just past the corpse of his vehicle a pair of mutant crow-men sat perched on the remains of a barbed-wire fence. This was a strange sight even here in this wilderness, and the only thing of note we had seen since the dead tree we had encounter more than an hour ago. They were monstrous configurations, the crow men: dark feathers giving way to sunburnt flesh. I didn't alert Jiminy to their presence.

This would have indeed wrongly upset the young man, and I needed him to take me to the end of the line for he was the map.

The creatures stared at me, amused for a moment, before one of them pulled out a cell phone. Strange, I thought. How could such a beast possess this technology? I thought at very least he may have carried a spiral notebook and when the moment came upon him, the wish to convey his thinking to the outside world, he would go to work with a pen, rip off the message he'd inscribed, fasten it to the leg above his fickle talons and then, as nature intended, take to the air and hand-deliver the message to its intended receiver. But this was evidently not the creature's custom. Lifting the device to the ear adjacent to his mangled features he placed a call. What was he saying I thought? In that moment I nearly panicked, suddenly seized by fear that he was sending word to those creatures with whom he shared his likeness that we were on the road, near death and ripe for devouring. I thought best not to disturb the driver with this inside knowledge; he would try to talk his way out of having his eyeballs eaten at another place in time.

The stranger introduced himself as Graham. He stood over six feet in brown and white button-up shirt with sweat circles occupying all the major crevasses. The same water responsible for this flowed steadily from his receding hairline over eyes that failed to blink and a smile that refused to falter. Where the brown lines of his shirt ended began brown pants, and there were moisture circles about his crotch that I supposed could have been sweat or urine, or perhaps a blending of the two. The crow-men finished their meeting and hopped off the wire fence. One flew away directly but the other hovered above Graham's car and took a shit on the windshield.

"Dirty bastard mutant," I called after it.

"When you gotta go, you gotta go," it squawked at me before flying away.

"That car has seen enough punishment today you freak scum."

"You talkin' to me buddy?" Graham asked. Though my outburst could have appeared to have been directed at him, I assured him it wasn't. Whether he believed me or not I don't know, but he asked if we could take him along the road till he told us to stop.

"What's the matter with you?" Jiminy was aggravated with me, I could tell. "Is this how you treat our guests? No wonder this journey has been so long and without merriment. You need to enhance your hospitality, my friend."

I accepted the fact that I may have been out of order but I was doing it for both their sakes. Once we reached our bitter end in this oblivion they might be the ones offering me a solemn apology, knowing then the kind of pressure I was under. Graham filled the back seat and we took off at high speed.

"When I was but a lad of eight and some I helped a woman give birth on this stretch. I had helped the old man do the same with calves and baby horses. So I was well prepared. It was a bad business. She was screaming and in quite a bit of pain. I was covered in blood and washed in mean spirit. So I slapped her across the face till she accepted the whole thing was going down."

This man we had found was the remedy to all our problems. His first story had taken by surprise and we relieved to be in the company of a trained medic should tragedy strike. Jiminy and I stared blankly out beyond the windshield and kept drinking as Graham spoke again.

"On a whim I once made love to, and subsequently wed, a woman who turned out to be a man. After the curious nature of our encounter we decided to set up a coffee shop in which Barry, which was her beautiful name, made sandwiches and bran muffins. One day I ate one of the muffins and was stapled to the shitter for three days together. On the four day, I filed for divorce."

This admission was enough for me to swallow hard and it forced Jiminy to spit out the mouthful of beer he was carrying. This man is a genius, I thought, a sage. I took out the small tape recorder in my pocket and made the decision to document this story, taking boldly the position as Graham's unofficial biographer.

"So how did your car break down," I asked the passenger. I hoped the crudeness of the question would not inhibit another great retort.

"I am on my way back from a bitter war and the weather report has me worried."

"Worried how?"

"It would seem that the human race has happened upon biblical times, and so I went to have a word with a man who knows about the severity of the situation. He said that my skills that I acquired in the navy, those directly relating to the designing and manufacturing of battleships will at last pay dividends. You see, son, I am in possession of one of the largest military contracts ever handed down to a civilian vendor. I have been tasked to deliver mankind from disaster, and so I am going to build the biggest damn boat you've ever seen."

I was suitably impressed but Jiminy was sceptical.

"I'm gonna call bullshit on that one, friend. You don't have the ingredients."

"Be silent, you fool – we are the presence of greatness!" I spoke as I shook a beer-clutching fist at the driver. "Would you like a beer?" I made our guest a reasonable offer.

"I gave up drinking around ought five. It seemed to rob me of my complexity and played havoc with my bowling average." Graham seemed to be on the verge of tears following this statement, but managed to shake it off and eventually asked us to pull over.

Before turning to walk away he gave us both a nugget of his remarkable gutter-philosophy for the road.

"If the red truck honks at you, honk back." Like all

108

good prophets he wandered back into the desert. Had I have been sober and in a better condition financially then I would have cried "fucking lunatic!" after him, but it was pity and a strong sense of what lay out there ahead of Graham that kept my tongue cemented. As we sped off I saw those freak crow bastards circling high over his head. The same one that had been talking on the phone earlier tipped a scraggy wing and let a globule of its by then fully processed lunch tumble out and streak toward the ground. The shit hit Graham, God's last ambassador, right on his bald patch. But this didn't stop him, he was fixed. He was a man on a mission just as we were. Hopefully for us, we didn't have that much farther to go.

~

At precisely 7:25pm when we pulled into the curb outside the unwholesome establishment known as the Rusted Rose. The wooden sign that hung over the door was held in place by a pair of shotgun shells decoratively repurposed, and it was the only saloon in 100 miles that still had batwing doors . . . this however was no real surprise. The gods in their wisdom had turned their backs on this town some time back in the middle ages; all that was left was the scratch'n'sniff end of society's dregs... and from the looks of it...all of them were present.

Five minutes' worth of wading through a sea of bodies that smelt like sweat, semen and a various assortment of cheap cologne, that was no doubt splashed aggressively over these angulating bodies by their owners in some half-assed, last ditch effort to camouflage the scent of the other two. By the time we arrived at the bar, so thoroughly baptised were we in the stench of the natives, we were automatically greeted as members of the tribe.

"Bring us six cold beers and a slightly chilled bottle of Wild Turkey," I said. The nubile young wench behind the bar was cute and desirable. Probably the reason she'd gotten the job in the first place. As I looked down the length of the bar I saw the dozen men seated there transform into ravenously vicious werewolves with magnificent erections plunging head-long into the walls of their pants. This girl was a fresh raw steak to them, and there'd be no call for the silverware or a napkin when the feasting commenced. It's not that they were aggressive about their intentions, though: rather they sat there quietly musing, the pornographic gyrations exploding within the confines of their brains only visible in their eyes.

"How chilled would you like the Turkey?" said the wench. It was a direct question phrased as a peculiar one.

"Just put six cubes of ice in two glasses," Jiminy said, "I need to use the men's room."

"It's the second door over by the back corner." The wench understood the layout, though it was impossible to see at this time and place in history. Save for those of us on stools by the bar the place was standing room only. I watched with generous anxiety as my friend braved the journey to relief himself. At that point I thought of spinning around quickly, calling for a napkin and a pen, composing a fitting epitaph to a brave man who only wanted to take a leak in the hour he met death.

My paranoia was running high. People all around were touching me. Granted most of this was accidental, but what if it wasn't? What if this is how they get you? How they slowly tenderise you, only after which do they lead you off into some nightmarish blind alley, beat you within an inch of your life and then kiss you on the cheek, hand you a bottle of modestly-priced champagne and marry you off to their barefoot daughters. Then you'd truly be a prisoner in this land. Thank god at that point the drinks arrived. I avoided the beer out of regard for the fact I may have to play getaway driver if the situation there went sour. I poured the Wild Turkey into both of the glasses filled with ice and consumed them both in quick succession. Blessed be your name Wild Turkey, yours is a siren song that lures me to my watery grave to which I succumb happily. For a moment, however brief, I felt at ease: The nefarious acts going on in the shadowy far reaches of the room, beyond the milling crowd, had no place in my thoughts. The strange soul-crushing retro-disco-techno music that was slowly sucking the intelligence from the establishment went mute and I found myself alone at last.

It was then I looked up at the clock, neon-lit and hanging over the bar. It shared real estate there with row upon row of bottles of gin and scotch. Intersecting these alcoholically fuelled super-highways were aging framed snapshots of the Rusty Rose's yesteryear. Turns out it may have been a hot ticket in a different age. At one point there had been some cosmic alignment and a celebrity vaguely reminiscent of a young George Hamilton had stopped by for refreshment on his road to riches and glory. But then my dream ended. I looked at the clock again and realised a great deal of time had passed since Jiminy had left the bar. Bravely I had to seek him out.

This was not the choice made by intellectual men I thought. I must be careful to study the floor before each step, my friend might just lie dead where he'd fallen – somewhere on the way to the men's room. So I filled my glass and left the bar, losing half of my drink when the first bohemian crashed into me. I wasn't angry at him for this. He was attempting an eclectic celebration of the dance, but was failing miserably.

A young woman grabbed my crotch when I found myself drowning in the thick of the crowd.

"Where are you from?" I heard faintly over the madness.

"Not from anywhere I expect to see again," was what escaped my lips.

"Would you like a blow job?"

This was a reasonable proposition, I told myself.

Perhaps it was customary in this place, and to refuse it I might be setting myself up for some horrible torture at the hands of the locals who look unfavourably upon those who look down upon the phrase, 'When in Rome...'

But this was no time for pleasure. I was locked on full search mode, and it was then that that which I was struggling to find found me. Jiminy appeared behind the woman. He was carrying a beer which he could not have gotten from the bar. That window was closed to us now, and I could only assume that he had stolen it from someone else while they were re-enacting a scene straight out of Sodom and Gomora, which I was highly appropriate given the nature of these surrounds.

"Hey that's my buddy, foul trollop," said Jiminy. In addition to the beer he had apparently acquired a Dickensian flair to his speech on his way back from the bathroom. But his attempt at affecting poetic style belied the crudeness of his next move. Jiminy grabbed the woman around the back of the neck, beneath her obnoxiously pink hair, and sent her flying toward the tavern wall. The crowd seemed to part for her like the Red Sea and it exposed a wall which was wood panelled half way up, meeting with an egg shell-coloured sheet-rock which continued onto the ceiling. There was a large poster advertising the same Funky Munky beer we had procured during our journey. The company had splashed out and gotten a real monkey to pose holding bottle of the product, cheekily grinning and giving the thumbs up. I know several prominent animal activists that would have spewed vitriolic hatred at such a campaign right before charging at the wall and ripping the poster down before burning it in effigy.

What you could not see directly, and especially lit by the putrid ambiance of the establishment was a shelf which protruded from the wall just as the wood panelling end and the sheet rock began. This woman who had wanted to lip-sync all over my pocket rocket collided with the shelf with her mid-section, letting fly with a banshee-like which caught the attention of the house security. One of these authorised security professionals were quickly on the scene. He clamped a hand down on Jiminy's shoulder.

"That was pretty funny sir, but I have to ask you to leave?"

Just live by the law I thought; the last thing we need is a brawl with people who are armed with more than strong drink. Jiminy had a thing about being touched like I did. I had witnessed a similar incident two nights ago when an unsuspecting old lady had tapped him on the shoulder to ask him for directions to the nearest phone booth while we were eating cheeseburgers on a park bench. She hadn't come through the experience well, I guess you'd say. I thought at the time she might have even needed medical attention, but Jiminy wrote her painful-sounding moans off as exaggerated attempts at getting more attention—and maybe a payoff—and insisted her wounds were at worst superficial.

"Let's not start a war with these people," I said calmly, "we have places to go."

Luckily my friend accorded at least some value to my input; otherwise nothing I said would have worked. There would been a battle royale if he'd had his way, and there would have been casualties. But we opted to finish our drinks and head outside. To my surprise we walked out of one crowd and directly into another.

The main thoroughfare was mostly dark but for the occasional streetlight. The world visible to us was at its brightest just out of the batwings of the Rusty Rose. Some electrical genius had lined florescent tubes around the perimeter of the building's awning which daggled over the sidewalk supported by ancient steel braces. But the crowd gathered beneath the harsh glow were not cavorting in a celebratory manner. We had entered the Colosseum and the Christians were being fed to the lions while the local law enforcement tried to hold back the chaos.

We had come late to these festivities and people were already beginning to walk away, except for a core group of around thirty civilians surrounding a police van. As we moved closer and from the cheap seats we saw that the cops had taken people into custody. These perps who had refused to come quietly red-faced with mace and handcuffed ready for the ride downtown. But the bus to the city had not yet departed. The cops were struggling with one assailant. This guy was over 7' 4", dressed like Herman Munster and in a mocking frame of mind. The boys in blue had the jewellery on one hand, but the other the giant held high above his head. He laughed at the law, who with all their weapons and tactical training could not get a hold of his other hand. I swear I even saw him laugh harder when they attempted to alter his personality with a little ride on the lightning.

"Just shoot the bastard in the knees," Jiminy suggested, "What were you issued guns for?"

To my surprise his admission was very clear, even beating out the noise from the tavern and the rowdy mob in the street. So timely was his delivery of the line that the crowd fell silent and all eyes focused on us. Don't do anything rash, if we stand still maybe they won't notice us, their visual acuity might be based of movement. If this was the case then the longer when remain frozen the better our chances of escape. But this thinking was optimistic. One of the cops then nodded in our direction.

"You two are next."

Next? Next in line to be beaten and handcuffed for the sin of trying to offer assistance? The vibrations were getting ugly; we needed an escape plan.

"Lord knows I do not want to be locked in a holding cell with Gigantor," said Jiminy. I assumed he was referring to the oversized comedian the cops were struggling with, and I got his point right away: If we were to be apprehended and placed in confinement with this colossus what then? Would he remember we had suggested the police use lethal force to subdue him, would he want revenge in the form of some vicious jail-cell sodomy? Our chances were slim if it came to preventing him from lavishing us with aggravated anal sex. We had to leave this place and soon. Our presence here was only causing problems. So we did the only thing we could think of at 2 a.m. . . . we went in search of a bakery.

~

We managed to slip away from the bad noise and the pleasant nature of the artificial and climate-controlled utopia of the bakery worked its magic to soothe our anxiety. Linger there for as long as possible I thought. Even though we had little interest in the plethora of baked goods on offer, we had to take advantage of the situation. We had narrowly avoided a terrible evening and sex in an uncomfortable setting.

Though we weren't really hungry we purchased warm rolls and Jiminy asked for a chicken pie. We found seats at one of the moulded white plastic settings among the friendly Rotarians. They were gathered there in impressive quantity considering the hour, all sipping coffee through false teeth, washing down jelly-filled pastries which added sweetness to their rancorous lives. Along the walls were photographic decals showing pictures of different shaped loaves of bread and bushels of wheat, as if those that ate here needed reminding of their food's origins. I was down two rolls when fresh coffee arrived. A genius thing this place was. You could eat in or takeaway. Like most franchises in this modern age this addition to the service was a plus. If you woke in the darkest hours before dawn and frantically realized you had no toast for breakfast, you could hurry out at speed. Then you didn't have to limit yourself. You could stand for as long as you liked in front of the hypnotic glass display cases and take your pick. A loaf of Wonder bread was no longer king of the food chain. Here there were assortments with herbs and concoctions with blends of bacon and cheese. We are spoiled for choice in this universe, but not today. At this hour we feasted and counted ourselves among the fortunate, for there was no telling what lay around the next curve on fate's gruesome highway.

"This is the most disgusting pie I have ever tasted," Jiminy said.

"Silence you cracked-brain simpleton, do you know how lucky we are to be welcomed here?"

A couple of the aging customers sitting close eyeballed us. What was it, I wondered? Was the attire we had chosen for the evening a fashion disaster? Were our table manners not making the grade? It is always difficult to eat in public; good etiquette takes time to master; after the first few times you pray that no one is scrutinising the way to chew or how you place the fork and knife back on the empty plate. Eventually all you need be concerned with is not forcing the food into your waiting gullet like a starving hyena having just stumbled on the corpse of a fallen wildebeest after days without solids. True starvation is indeed an excuse to abandon decorum, granting you full permission to shove as much food into your pie hole as possible with stained and desperate fingers. But this wasn't really that, and either way I couldn't see where Jiminy or I had degenerated to the behaviour of hungry animals. So to my mind those accusing eyes were out of order.

"These senior citizens are judging us," I said. "We need to change our tact."

"Tell them to go fuck themselves," said Jiminy.

Despite having assessed it as grotesque, he was wolfing down the pie, and he'd spat that last suggestion out through a mouthful of it with such style and so pointedly that I figured the gawkers had gotten the point without my having to make any more of it.

This being the case we ordered the next round of coffee to go. The waitress was another short beautiful woman not unlike the one in the tavern. Is this where all the splendid creatures of this world have vanished to, I was wondering — are they all clerks strolling this catwalk of enticement? If that was in fact the case, then I needed to get out more. My monastic literary banishment from the world suddenly seemed trite and boring and in desperate need of coming to a merciful end. With inducements like this comely thing serving beer and food, no wonder my inspiration had dried up. I resolved in that instant to eat out more and to visit random stores with absolutely no shopping agenda. At last I saw a way back into society's wheel. Time to get that big bastard spinning hard and fast.

~

When we walked back out into the street the circus was still in town. The law had given up on trying to properly restrain the behemoth and now they were just forcibly cramming him into the van with little or no regard for their own personal safety. It was a reckless plan, but with the entire force on hand and enough firepower at their disposal to close down the city and declare martial law, the big guy who still seemed in possession of his good humour was enjoying the whole experience far too immensely to pause and take human life.

"Shoot that Sasquatch and be done with it," said Jiminy.

Had my friend not learned from past experience? His words again managed to make us the center of attention, and my feet felt like they were suddenly coated in cold concrete. Like the guy who knew too much in some late night noir, I stood there mentally preparing myself to be dropped into the nearest deep body of water for simply being in the wrong place at the wrong time — with the wrong loudmouthed companion. Any serious student of those fables observed during the hours of insomnia knows that you never plead for your life. Instead you offer a silent prayer and try to make an honest getaway. This course was still open to us. Though we were ignorant of the advanced geography of the city, we had nothing ahead of us. We could run like Butch and Sundance and just keep going. Sure, the super-posse they'd likely send out would undoubtedly catch up with us eventually, but not before we had made the headlines, making them earn their night's salary and buying ourselves another few hours of revelry.

Two cops broke away from trying to stuff the big guy into the van and came straight toward us. Jiminy panicked and ran over to a taxi that had just pulled up to the curb. And even though three people had just entered and filled the backseat, my friend didn't care. Arriving at the still open back door, he threw himself inside and ended up sprawled across the laps of all three.

The old cabby was not a good-humoured character. This was a man at the end of his shift and in no mood for my friend's impromptu acrobatics. Jiminy rolled over on his bed comprised of three sets of trembling knees and pronounced his destination.

"GET US THE FUCK OUTTA HERE, STAT!"

The people-mattress my friend had used to cushion his fall was comprised of a man and two prostitutes. While still drinking coffee on the sidewalk I could have sworn I saw the exit a chinses restaurant three storefronts down from the bakery. The man was dressed in what appeared to be a hired tuxedo and the hookers came in sequence blue and red with cosmetics on their faces to hide even the most stubborn blemish or livid scar. As they had walked toward the curb the man had crabbed both their asses blatantly. They were enjoying his company far too much to be casual acquaintances, and no one sports that much make-up unless they are trying to conceal the gender they used to be. I deduced they were working girls from the sheer fact that both the dinner and the ride were relatively cost efficient. His character would need every cent he had once they got to wherever they were going. Nothing beyond the regular party was going to be on the menu with this guy's wallet. There would be nothing kinky and there would certainly be no seconds on this night. This guy's bank was stretched to breaking point. The last thing he needed now was the cab fare to be run up be some drunken hoodlum who could keep his mouth shut.

"I'm not taking you anywhere, so fuck off!" said the cabby to my severely anxious compadre. Fuck off does mean simply go away, it means fuck off; it leaves no manoeuvring space for the imagination. It is the apotheosis of stern commands when someone else's presence is definitely hampering the natural order of things. Some customer who is strongly opposed to buying the metaphorical t-shirt you are trying to push on them, then – off you must fuck.

Jiminy was receiving no quarter from his enemies on this night. He'd made a few brand new shit lists, and once you go down in those books, it's very difficult to get back in the black. You have to be hopeful, kamikaze and possess no fear of the inevitable in attempting to regain favour with those whose images you have tarnished. It is imperative at times to stop, take a moment and mentally compose a fitting tribute, or your own epitaph depending on which way the conversation goes. Needless to say with beleaguered confidence my friend crawled grudging out of the taxi, and with the police nipping at our heels we ran off into the night like a pair of well-seasoned criminals having escaped the gallows.

After half an hour we had no more juice left. The

invincibility supplied us by the liquor we carried was weakening in effect and we were quickly converting back into mortals. So, seeing that no one had followed us, we sat in the gutter and tried at least to regain our breath.

It was there that we were joined by a character in the remnants of a three-piece suit. He had seemingly materialised out of thin air, but when he puked at our feet we knew him to be one of us, another of God's Distinct Prototypes. He referred to himself as Freddo, best we could tell, but he was in a worse state than we were so he could have said something else. As we would be well on our way by dawn the name his mother gave him was of little consequence, still it helps to get a response out of people if you can garner their attention first by speaking their name.

"My best friend just got married. I and about a dozen other guys here have already slept with the bride so there is an awkwardness in the room. You boys want to come back in for a drink?"

He stumbled back into the bushes behind us and vanished like Shoeless Joe Jackson.

"This is fantastic. Fortune favours us indeed," said Jiminy, and he charged off toward where Freddo had disappeared a mere few seconds earlier.

I followed, pushing my way through the dense undergrowth till I uncovered the makings of a well-manicured lawn which blanketed the grounds surrounding a house straight out of Gone with the Wind. All it was missing was a demented Irish patriarch on a rocking chair happily cradling a double-barrel shotgun.

To one side of the house a large white tent had been erected, and those gathered within were being entertained by disco lights and music from a bygone era. As I approached, Jiminy came rushing out to greet me with a cold can of beer and a glass of whiskey.

"There is more where that came from," he told me. "Quick, we need to take advantage of this situation."

As I entered the tent with him I saw the remainder of the wedding party. The bride and groom it would seem had long since departed. At this point the floor was apparently open to a screeching mob of fools that hadn't been made aware that disco had been sent to its eternal rest several decades ago. The revellers had been at it a while from the looks of it, and most of them were thus no longer "disco neat and tidy": Most of the man sat slouched at tables, trading loud burps and sex stories as they lounged in torn white shirts with loose bow-ties and an assortment of food wine and barf stains over black chinos. The women, all dancing with martini and wine glasses full of that which had rendered them shabby princesses were out in the middle of the floor, bright, chirpy and cheerful like a convention of fading beauty queens who were out trying to recapture some of their old thunder.

We sat at a table with Freddo, who produced several quarts of rum and a dozen or more cans of beer.

"You know you look real familiar. Do I know you?" he asked me.

"I don't see how you could. I'm not part of this community." I told him the truth. I knew what Jiminy had planned when he came waltzing out of the tent holding liquor. He was out to deceive these drunken idiots so that we might regain our former glory on his dime. That plan sat difficultly with me. I was happy to have one for the road before we hit it again, but I saw Jiminy's eyes. He was settling in, he wanted me to build the facade while he lived it up like one of the family.

It was then was then that one of the drunks thought he recognised me.

"It's Toby isn't it? Fucking Toby, it's been twenty years. Tell me what happened to you. Marcelle, come quick – it's Toby!"

His cry went out, and the next thing I knew one of the inebriated fairy queens was hanging over my left shoulder. She smelt uncomfortably of dying roses, the scent that grandmothers of the world dowse themselves with to cover the sickening scent of mothballs. Her makeup was running as though she had been decorated with wax crayons and spent fleeting spritzes beneath a blowtorch.

"Toby it IS you. Where have you been? How is Camille, is she with you?"

Jiminy winked at me from behind the glass of scotch he was drinking. I took this to be my cue. Don't panic. Be creative. They obviously haven't seen this guy Toby in years, and the best advantage you have is that they're no longer in command of their senses. Take a deep breath. Channel the spirit of this stranger. Let him speak to them.

"Yeah, I moved west. And Camille has been dead for about three weeks."

That wasn't calm, it was full of panic. What if in some strange ironic twist, Toby and Camille suddenly walked into the room in the next moment, surprising everyone? Then we'd be picking up the tab again. That would be strike three and this is the last inning. We won't be able to shake this one clear like all the others. I have used fake identities before, but only in matters of extreme personal danger. But I was not under threat here. Despite their dress and taste in music, I liked this situation. The vibrations were steady and strong but now Jiminy had set me up for failure. This singular performance could be our ticket back into the light. It all fell on my shoulders and I felt heavy and in need of a lot more rum. So I opened the closest bottle and began to tell dead men's tales.

And everything was going well. I was deep into the act and proving I had lived many past lives when some backseat fascist decided to bring the curtain down on our act. He approached Freddo and started throwing the book at him. Turns out this was a private event, and those not properly dressed and without the proper credentials were persona non grata; in short, we would need to make ourselves scarce. The fascist, however, was not all stick. He allowed us to take the beers in our hands and finish the rum in our glasses. Jiminy decided to run a little interference while I requisitioned one of the unopened bottles of rum from the table. Smart move I thought, we still had many miles to travel and there was no telling what encounters lay ahead of us and how dark and deep we would have to plunge till sunup. Jiminy, like Judas before him, kissed the fascist of the cheek. As hard as the man was, he took it with a smile and Jiminy tucked another stolen liquor bottle under his arm. We headed out without fanfare; we had been welcomed as returning heroes on the way in, but this was different. Had we had invitations the situation might have been different, but this was the best we could hope for. This brief detour had yielded some good things, but it was time to get back on our lonely trek. We could only hope that our next stop was a peaceful one. It had been a full 76 hours since either of us had gotten any sleep; we were running on stolen rum and pure adrenalin.

~

This part of the evening was the coolest the weather had been all day. It was hypnotic, and we both felt that primal urge to take off all of our clothes and howl at the moon, offering up some loud violent prayer to whatever forces controlled the weather.

Two clicks down the road we took we came across the long forgotten warning signs of mass civilisation; far from the intermittent pockets we had thus encountered. There several blocks of fading duplexes which seemed out of place in this Hades landscape. The pruned hedges that marked the property lines implied a hint of sophistication on the part of the dwellers that lay like slumbering content cavemen next to their cheating wives and homicidal teenagers. In the valley of the blind the one-eyed king had deserted the throne, and now these - his once oppressed and marginalised subjects - were ruling the land. We had to walk softly through this part of town. There is nothing worse than the uncaged fury of a vicious suburbanite woken before his wristwatch dictates. If roused at this hour, they would come at us with everything they had. There would garden hoses and kitchen implements used for procedures not listed in their instructions. We had to be on guard and not take any step lightly.

Soon we came to a four-way intersection and that's where we met the last horseman of the apocalypse.

He was a 6'5" African-American who looked like he would scare the living shit any small animal in the neighbourhood. Yet he was well dressed in a pressed and laundered Nike tracksuit and Italian-made leather sandals.

"Hey, name's Curly Sugar Rivers."

His voice was all-the-way Barry White and he flashed a full Arlington Cemetery of pearly well-kept teeth at us.

"You boys drink wine?"

"You bet, guv'nor," said Jiminy. My friend seemed at ease in the stranger's presence but I was not all the way convinced. I have nothing against people of colour, let's get that straight right now; but this man was standing around far too casually at this ungodly hour to be without some dark purpose. This had all the hallmarks of being some crossroads deal with the devil and we were out of chips. Even if the house lent us a marker we were still in over our heads. The cards had been cold the last couple of hands and it was only foolish courage now that was allowing us not to fold.

"I keep a sensational cellar, and I live close by," Rivers said, "that is, if you don't mind walking a little further?"

This surely couldn't be the ending we were hoping for. This neighbourhood was the last known refuge of this world's cream of the crop. If we gained admission and they turned us loose inside they might expect us to deliver. They would sit us down and expect answers to all the hard questions. We would need time to process the messages they were sending us, and in turn, we would need more than microwave karma. They were expecting communication from the powers that control the great magnet, and I knew we were not the heralds this culture was counting on. We were not the resurrection and the life, but rather inconvenient hush and bullshit that sold humanity on the idea that the civilized shall inherit the wind.

"Naturally it would be impolite if we don't go and have one drink," my friend said.

You've had too much to drink already you poor fool. Indeed we both had. But I knew there would be no convincing him otherwise. I could have let Jiminy go on alone while I contemplated my future staring up at the stars and staying on point with the last of the rum in the bottle. But if he ran into trouble, and Rivers turned out to be the malevolent Samael I took him for, then I would have blood on my hands. I knew that with no soap or towel I would find myself at the heart of the Scottish play and have his accusing ghost haunting me at every turn.

So, somewhere between certain and indecision, I followed my eager friend to his doom. We walked for about a block till we came to a low-set brick dwelling that looked like a miniature of the Playboy Mansion. Rivers opened the front door of Ursa Major on a budget and we slipped through to the interior.

His living room was something out of a Wilt Chamberlain home catalogue complete with a framed team photo of the 1973 San Diego Conquistadors hanging above a jaguar skinned-covered sofa.

"Have a seat, I'll be with you directly," said Rivers before he disappeared into another room.

"His is none too shabby old sport," said Jiminy.

Had it regressed to Gatsby so soon? I thought we had

at least another hour before that coach became a pumpkin. Drink up quickly I thought, show what a reckless alcoholic you are. Luckily I had the rum to quell my paranoia. Rivers had been gone for the length of a bible. No way had he simply slipped away to the kitchen for three glasses and a bottle of his own blood which he would force us to suck down, turning us into the devil's concubines like himself.

When he finally came back the rum was gone and I was on the verge of panic. Jiminy punched me in the shoulder and tried to reason with me.

"Is this how you behave in public you fucker? Try not to spill any on this couch, it is prohibitively expensive."

My Conscience spoke more than truth. Rivers' furniture was not something you came across at any of the mass-market homeware superstores that dotted the land near all the major metropolises. This stuff was custom, refined, each piece probably the only one of its kind. I was pouring sweat. My blood is too thick to deal with this kind of pressure, but the fake fire was burning and the air conditioning was on the crest of blowing out snowflakes. So it is to be psychological breakdown. We were indeed in perilous territory now, and just to add spice to our demise the seating was insanely comfortable. But that was the greatest trick the devil ever pulled. He was able to convince the human race that Hell wasn't so bad because there you would enjoy every earthly vice in copious amounts. From high-class call girls that didn't want your money to expertly crafted club sandwiches. This was the slow descent, and the cork was yet to exit the bottle.

Rivers sat before us cross-legged on a pink shag rug beneath a glass and chrome coffee table upon which he placed three glasses.

"I trust these will not offend your palette. I prefer drinking from brandy glasses but it's the maid's day off."

"Why not," I found myself saying, "they seem as

reasonable a place to pour booze as any."

He uncorked the wine and rested the gaping wound against the tip of his nose before brandishing a grin that could make you forgive any person for tearing out the still-beating heart from your chest and asking if your preference was medium or well done.

"This is a '41 Sauvignon," Rivers sounded proudly.

I knew that should mean something to us but it didn't. Truth is I was becoming very cynical when it came to classy beverages. Anything that was over $1000 a sip seemed to make me uncomfortable for the person bold enough to bring the bottle to the table. He had to be aware that the second he left the room we going to set upon it like the vampires we had recently become. We would need more than a single pour, which went without saying. But to give the man credit he filled our glasses halfway without batting an eyelid.

O' damn you, you bastard, this stuff is good. It made me drop whatever heavy artillery I was carrying and forced me to make light of my eventual execution and just accept things. I thought perhaps my friend might escape this web of pleasure with the remainder of the bottle the second our host took to me with a machete or some ornamental samurai sword. He would wander the lands of luxury till after breakfast and then alert the authorities. This could have been wishful thinking. But I knew the sight of me being prepared for a Tibetan burial would awaken the honest blue collar blood in him. There's no way that man would stand for such atrocities, no matter how willingly we had invited them in for an opulent pre-dawn drinking binge.

It was 4:00 a.m. when Jiminy said,

"Hey Sugar, I have to use your bathroom."

Rivers told my friend it was in the back, four doors down the hall on the left. He rose quickly and managed not to create havoc. Very impressive I thought, considering the amount of alcohol the man had in his system.

Left to our own devices and with the expensive wine coursing through my veins I thought it best to explain the situation. After all we were guests in this man's place; he might wish to know the nature of the trouble he had invited.

"So I guess you are curious about the nature of our mission?"

"You talk if you like, baby, I'm here to listen," Rivers said. By the look in his eyes I'd have to say he was teetering on the brink of disinterest, but his courtly manners prevented him from simply saying shut the fuck up and have another drink.

I explained that we had received a phone call two days prior while drinking on a small rooftop bar in a house of ill repute known as the Malt Caravan. It was this New Age spin on the old-fashioned beer and burger joint that had been the financial collaboration between an over-enthusiastic used car salesman and the local outlaw biker gang that had cooked it up as a front to hide the profits from their drug-running game. It had opened nearly eight months behind schedule when the petty rural excuse for government made it difficult for them to obtain certain building permits. But those bastards met with the swift justice all small town bureaucrats do when they ludicrously assume that telling leatherclad, knife-swallowing Hell's Angels that enough is enough, hoping that will make them back down and take up crocheting. The bikers made sure all opposed didn't have their votes counted and the place opened with s flurry of press and parties, although this only lasted a few weeks after the real people that made the little world turn, Joe and Judy Average, woke up to the fact that $70 for a cheese burger and a Budweiser was too rich for a Friday evening.

We took to the roof because they wouldn't let us smoke inside. We were a pack in and $200 down in imported ale when Jiminy's cell phone signalled the helicopters coming in out of the rising sun with Bill Kilgore in command looking for his first whiff of napalm in the morning.

"You'll have to do the talking, I'm too drunk," Jiminy said handing me the phone.

The voice at the other end said something about being guests at a birthday party and how it was imperative that we make an appearance. Though this Ghost of Christmas Future knew my friend was drowning in the sauce, he told me to pass him the phone to arrange accommodation. After five minutes the call was over, the cigarettes were all gone and our drinks were dry.

"We'll take my car. But first we'll need to stop by a store because I suddenly feel the urge for pickles." Jiminy had his faults, but I was not prepared to sit idly by and watch any man starve to death.

So we took off in the clothes we had on. We picked up more beer and cigarettes, and a case of whiskey on the side. We were nearly arrested at the supermarket trying to buy the pickles when Jiminy confessed an urgent need to shit and attempted to banish this demon in one of the oversized potted plants the store used as beautification. Then we pulled into some lonely parking lot and drank half the beer before getting the last sleep we would know for many hours.

My audience's face was awash with confusion. I had not managed to give a good account of ourselves. This journey had been frightening, with overtones of extreme persistent drinking. But still Rivers sat there quietly listening, waiting. Maybe he was trying to get it all squared away in his head before he chose to comment. Maybe he had nothing to offer at all. For what could he do for us to help the cause to which we had dedicated ourselves? He could lock us in some grim lonely room with no windows and refuse us any more drink till we agreed to stop and breathe, to take the world and everything we had yet to accomplish with a degree of seriousness that we were yet to put into action.

"HELP, HELP, JESUS FUCKING CHRIST, HELP. SHE WANTS TO LICK MY ASSHOLE!"

My Conscience came running through the living room screaming. He cleared the coffee table with a leap that had all the grace of a mountain goat.

He was out the door and screaming in the street when a tall, blonde, female bodybuilder, naked but for a pair of high heels and a matching black satin bath robe came strolling in his wake.

"Well I didn't expect that," she said.

Then she looked down at me and our eyes met.

"Oh well," she continued, "I guess you'll have to do."

She flexed muscles covered liberally in tanning cream and baby oil as she approached. Her pussy was shaved and her chest was tight as a snare drum except for the small portions of her breasts at the base of her pectorals, which flapped about carelessly.

"Rhonda, these are our guests." Rivers acquired his feet and tried to reason with her. She wasn't interested and slapped the big man unconscious.

At that point I took the initiative and got the fuck outta Dodge. I had no desire to have my anus treated in any fashion that it hadn't already become accustomed to. It was a holy place and an exit only. I used it for shitting and occasionally hiding loose change when the situation called for it. I was not going to submit to this She-Hulk and let her use my third eye as some kind of theme park attraction. Besides, I was tired. The night had gone on for longer than I predicted, and sex oral or anal with Hercules' twin sister was not what the fortune teller saw in the cards for me. All I wanted now was a place to rest and recuperate. I had seen the dark underbelly of the human condition and all I wanted was to take a shower, possibly a warm bath. This adventure had worked me over and I was already mentally violated by the proceedings. The physical equivalent would have to wait until Rivers regained consciousness. But perhaps this woman's eagerness had gotten the best of her. I saw in her eyes that she craved her fetish and I believe that our well-dressed host was going to service her needs whether he consented or not. But this was a matter they would have to work out between themselves. My friend was out there and screaming like a madman, having found his cell door unlocked and the stuffed animal at the foot of his bed telling him to 'run' for no justifiable reason. He needed my counsel, and I was not hanging around this house, as magnificent as it was, to witness the unbridled concupiscence that was about to be placed on the menu.

~

It was my friend's continued cries for help that aided me in tracking him down. Had he not been mentally obliterated by the fear of having a female bodybuilder shoving her tongue into his ass, he might still be out there, lost to all knowledge.

Across a short wooded area I saw him kneeling down.

"What are you doing? That beast is still indoors, probably sodomizing that classy character with his own penis. There is no reason to hide in there." I tried to keep my tone even and civil. No reason to traumatise this poor man any further I thought. The mere prospect of becoming Queen Kong's sex slave was a harrowing proposition of its own.

"The motel we have a room at is just through these trees." He sounded calm, but his refusal to step out from the trees told me was still a prisoner of his dread. I started walking through the woods. The going was simple at first, but as I drew closer to Jiminy's position I had noticed the ground softening rapidly. What had been solid had quickly become mucky and dismal. A number of times I struggled to lift my feet and at one point I felt my shoe being pulled away from my foot. Slow and easy, I thought. Who knows what lies beneath the surface? The creatures that dwelt in such swampy terrain were not to be trifled with. Most of them were passive, but the predators were extremely cunning. The beasts would lie in wait. They had the patience of a serial killer who had particular tastes and would stalk their victims, watching from the dark, studying habits, living only for the opportune moment to strike.

It felt as though I was wearing shoes cast in solid iron. Each step was an odyssey. When I finally came to Jiminy it took several minutes to free him from the swamp's vice-like grip, as he had almost been sucked down to his knees. It was a slow, laborious process, but eventually we dug ourselves free.

We came out of the trees and into a neon sunrise. A giant lavender sign that proclaimed The Venture Motor Inn towered before us like the statue of some Egyptian god. Its glow was piercing but welcoming. Thank heaven. We had stumbled upon our salvation completely by accident. The promise of a soft place to rest our battle-scarred bodies, and a daily-cleaned bathroom with complimentary hand wash and toothpaste had kept us from slipping and completely surrendering to fear and loathing. We might have given up and simply thrown our bodies into the road hours ago if the promise of this end had not been cemented in our minds.

The Inn consisted of eight cabins, all neatly aligned. The exterior of the building was predominantly white but for the doors to the rooms and the gutters on the roof. To keep the whole place in line with a common theme, these were painted the same lavender as the sign. This place was most likely run by a husband and wife duo, and the man of the house, in order to keep his spot in the matrimonial bed, had succumbed to his wife's ideas relating to the visual aesthetic of the establishment.

We tried not to make any noise and we thought we had succeeded. My friend had produced a room key that I didn't even know he had and we were almost through the door of the cabin when nasty vibrations began swooping and screeching and diving all around us. These took the form of coarse language being hurled at us like stones by the owner of the motel. She of the lavender décor stood there dressed in a robe and sporting hair curlers of the same colour. This was the woman in charge all right, that much was certain. Now all we had to do was win her favour so we could go inside and shower, leaving the hell hounds in the street. God knows there were victims aplenty they could enjoy in our absence.

"You will not be going into that cabin wearing those trousers," she said to Jiminy. "What the heck happened to those pants anyhow?"

The owner was referring to the dark muddy residue of the swamp, which had almost completely altered the nature of my friend's chinos.

"Don't know," he said, "I think I shit myself."

This statement could partly have been fact. I held not a doubt in my mind that when Jiminy had been confronted with Conan's sister's sexual desires not an hour ago, he may have indeed panicked and let part of him go, giving birth to his own litter of smelly little turd babies. This could have also been part of his reasoning for heading into deepest part of the swamp. He perhaps saw it as adopting a kind of natural camouflage. It would not have masked the odour, but it had the ability to divert insult from gross injury.

The lady in lavender walked away when my friend dropped his pants, strode over and threw them in an obliging dumpster. I didn't wait. I went into the cabin, shed my soiled garments and took to the shower. The bathroom was a blinding white all over, and my eyes strained to cope with the intense nature of its brilliance. But the water pressure was just as strong and the glory of the warm water returned my strength. This was indeed the budget-chain fountain of youth, and the longer I basked in it, the better I felt.

I took down one of the towels with the motel's name emblazoned on it and wrapped it around my waist. Next stop was the bed. I had read some place that the sheets in these places might have been rotated reasonably often but the decorative bed covers were seldom treated to as thorough a regime. But I didn't give a shit. I was beyond my capabilities and had been so for several days. All I wanted now was the sleep of a stone. I fell hard upon the mattress and found it to be surprisingly soft. Many nights had I slept in similar establishments where the bedding felt what I imagine the comfort of a coffin to be like. This of course never really concerns people when making a selection. When you are finally placed into that eternal lodging you are beyond filling out a complaint form. The endless sleep requires no late checkout or fear of being overcharged for the use of the mini-bar or the in-house movies. In that state everything is first class, and all you need do is ride the warm light to the other side, where hopefully the reservations have been made well in advance.

Strange memories in this byzantine darkness on the outskirts of God's nowhere. But that is all about to change. Sunrise is almost upon us and soon there'll be a knocking at that tiny portal by the door. It will be opened from the outside and a tray with silver-domed lids masking the cholesterol city we call breakfast will serve to revitalise us further. It will come with cold orange juice and hot coffee and only then will we be fully resurrected.

I was drifting off to sleep when Jiminy finally came back into the room. There must have been a stiff breeze blowing outside, for it brought a faint cloud of dust and the smell of stale spaghetti into the room. My friend had been gone, it seemed, for an eternity. This didn't make sense. The dumpster had only been a short walk away, out by the road under the sign. What trouble could have

134

found its way into our lives across such a short, reasonably friendly space?

"What took you so long, and why do you smell like overcooked pasta?" I asked without moving or opening my eyes.

"I threw my cell, wallet and my lucky Budweiser belt buckle into the trash with the pants. I was half way back to the room before I saw the error of my ways and had to turn back. Had to go fishing."

I had hoped he might have showered before falling asleep but he didn't. Such was the way of this. It brought memories of when we once attended a soiree during the flair of our youth. My friend had his eye on this truly picturesque, raven-haired beauty. She was an earthly angel if ever there was one. All he wanted was to dance with her, so I slipped her a few bucks and told her to give him his money's worth. In the end she gave me back the cash and told me my friend was a real sweetheart. She said he might actually have a better shot at a lifelong romance if only he'd had a bath before positioning her. This was not his way. When you grow up in a dry land where water is a luxury, every drop must be accounted for. This was three summers and a thousand years ago. He'd had access to washing facilities since then, yet the old wisdom was too deeply ingrained. All those years in the desert had forged a different kind of superhuman. One that didn't hit the showers until people complained about the smell.

But my head was empty and I let sleep take a seat at the controls. I hoped I would get a few hours at least on autopilot. Enough time to compartmentalise and fortify the outer wall. I knew my battle with the world was far from over. I had survived yet another skirmish, but the enemy's troops were still there, out beyond the wire with their war-faces fixed and their bloodstained teeth hankering for refreshment. But that was all in the future now, and I was not there yet. I would take some time to swap stories with the ancestors. Get the lowdown on everything I'd be doing wrong and perhaps even a few handy tips or some mystical twelve step program to set things to right. But for now silence, stillness. Only after a healthy dose of it would this man born into battle shake off yesterday and get his ass out of bed, get back on the eternal wheel. The momentary quiet before the storm was great – till it all begins again.

AUTHOR'S NOTE FROM KENT HILL

It is presumptuous indeed to think one could capture the music of a literary giant.

At minimum, all one can strive for is to capture their rhythm. I have in the past attempted to do so with those authors whom have captured my imagination and admiration. Authors like Lansdale, Kuttner and Bukowski. But, I admit, there was something that always made me hesitate trying to try on the shoes of Hunter Thompson. For one, he had a music all his own; a music that was cultivated by his life and the way he lived it. Two, he was a reporter, a chronicler of situations, people and times – and it's hard to find that magic on the page if your own life doesn't in some way share elements of crossover.

As good as one can become, there are people for their time and place. Hunter Thompson came to prominence in a time of great change and upheaval. The persona and the writer at its core blended together and formed the Gonzo-eye view of the world. He placed himself at the heart of the narrative, and though fuelled by earthly vices, his elegant prose rose to the surface; adding a beauty to the tragedy and decay he saw in the decline and eventual death of the American dream.

He didn't go out on top, but some might say he went down swinging.

Not a bad way to go.

-- *Kent Hill*

Kevin Candela

Day Seven.

I'm starting on Day Seven because I didn't know what was happening the previous six. My mind was rebelling. Reptile Brain was right but denial is a potent barbiturate and my head was wallowing in it. All the signs were there and RB was screaming, or more accurately hissing, "It's true whether you like it or not."

Do I like it?

I'm not answering that without my attorney.

Let's backtrack so this sounds a little less like the ravings of a madman, even though I now freely acknowledge it might be just that.

Let's go back to Day One.

~

Day One.

That's the day I visited that sanctuary on the Big Island. The day I first manifested what I've come to think of as pure, unadulterated spirit possession, no less.

The day I saw *her*.

I was in Hawaii on business. Nothing fits America's Stolen Paradise quite like a bunch of suits stomping all over it, sucking down liquor and designer drugs and staggering around like the New Kings of Owyhee we all think we are when the chemicals are racing hard enough and the tropical sun is French frying our synapses through the tops of our carefully coiffed skulls.

To be fair I'm not a very impressive suit. I sell pools and spas and it looks bad in our biz if we meet someplace non-photogenic. Last year we'd done Colorado – the Rockies – and I'm wondering now if my temporary proximity to Aspen had anything to do with all this extreme weirdness. But no digression: this is a mission.

So there we were – time on our hands after doing little but sitting and listening all day – and I said screw this and took off in the Lexus rental. Ostensibly my plan was to walk one of those ancient lava tubes, but I got diverted by a sign for the sanctuary I'd read about in a favorite book of mine.

That's when it happened.

And I'm pretty sure the Hawaiian deity Lono had something to do with it, because his name is in the title of that book. I'll get back to this.

The site itself isn't much to look at. But that didn't matter because I didn't look around. I felt different the moment I laid eyes on it, and I've felt that way ever since.

I can't describe the change. Not even now. I just remember feeling weird, like I had been expected and shown up and something was going on but I was out of the loop as to what it was.

And the next thing I knew my Lexus was being swarmed by enormous bats.

I didn't even know Hawaii had them. I guess it makes sense – lava tunnels are caves, bats like caves – but these were no ordinary cheep-cheep-cheeps that flap past in the dark. These were like those huge fruit bats you see two poor dirty swamp workers in cracked sepia-toned photos stretching out like a tarp between them. Two of them were enough to blind me completely as they flopped their fat rat bodies across my windshield and others thrashed away relentlessly at the rich man's obscenity around me. I had to hit the brakes and I did so ruing that whole "take a side road, see some fun stuff" decision because a back road in the jungle at night is no time to be under attack by bats big enough to eat your face.

I slammed on the brakes, threw the Lexus into park and looked into the back seat. The fanny-loving TSA had of course left me traveling bereft of any sort of defenses, not that my mind worked that way at this time a week ago anyway.

That's come along since.

I had mace but that wasn't going to scare off these savage bastards from the looks of it. They were determined. Mad, almost. I could hear teeth clicking on glass as they tried to get a good bite into that stubborn material to open up my black candymobile and enjoy its chewy center.

I hit the horn. Long and hard.

Lame. When did they emasculate horns? I wrote off a lot of money to rent that thing.

The bats didn't care. They were seriously not quitting. And I wasn't going anywhere.

If this all sounds like a lot to buy, consider that I heard not one but two Doppler Effect blasts from the horns of other vehicles as they shot by me. I guess I can't say I wasn't surprised that they didn't stop and help because it's hard to picture what they were looking at. Not sure I'd have stopped either: A car covered in giant bats really isn't a fair challenge for a novice Good Samaritan.

Leaning over the seat, I fumbled with my briefcase and suitcase and soon found myself pissed once again that the damned airline pigs had confiscated my sports air horn. That might have chased the dogged beasts away, I was thinking. But maybe not. They were tenacious.

And then they were gone.

~

I only saw her for a moment, because that's as long as she was there. I think.

I was looking out of the windshield through smears of bat slobber, so details were sketchy. She had long jet black hair, was wearing some kind of dark one piece skin or something more Native American than Hawaiian, and —oh yeah—her eyes were glowing bright green.

She was standing about thirty feet in front of the car, right dead center between the headlight beams, and looking right at it. At *me*, I figured, although I couldn't tell which way those freak orbs were staring through the bat goo.

And then she was gone too. I could have sworn she just faded away.

I got back to the hotel well after midnight, but there was no way I was going to sleep after that experience. I headed down to the lounge after a quick clothes change and, in doing so, brought the weirdness virus I'd contracted at the sanctuary with me.

The lounge opened out onto the pool and surrounding courtyard. I ordered a neat whiskey double, fired it down to settle my nerves, repeated as required and then took a third off with me to check out the late night crowd.

The myth: Beautiful saleswomen shed their inhibitions and skinny dip together late at night in resort pools.

The reality: Pool is empty and dead still and the handful of folks lurking around said locale at one in the morning are either dealing drugs, buying them or desperately contemplating the bad moves they'd already made on vacation and trying to figure out if that itch was

142

just an allergic reaction to hotel laundry detergent.

From the looks of him, Spanster would have been firmly in that third category.

Ward Philip Spanster: A great bear of a man, robust and charismatic and quite incapable, I soon discovered, of speaking in anything remotely resembling a hushed voice.

"Sit down, son," he told me.

I have no idea why I did.

But I set myself down on the chaise lounge next to the tortured deck chair that was struggling mightily to keep his girth in its confines. I didn't stretch out, just nodded where I sat, tipped my drink at him and fired it down.

"Spanster's the name," he said. "And before you say it I know: You didn't ask."

"I would have," I told him. "Given time."

He grinned—looked like an ogre smiling at his dinner —and I just smiled back at him, figuring he was the type that wanted to talk and didn't expect too much feedback.

"You're all right," he said. "Whatcha drinkin'?"

I held up my glass, cocked my head at it and stared at the ice cubes.

"Looks like...nothing," I said.

"That won't do at all," he said, and he turned and hollered over at the bar before I knew what was happening. "Hey!" he bellowed so loudly it rattled second floor windows. "How about we get a bottle over here for my buddy."

Great. I was his buddy. I'd had brand new buddies before. It's a hit and miss, mostly miss, proposition.

My pessimism abated when the bottle arrived. Bottles weren't allowed away from the bar.

"You've got some pull," I said as Alanda, who I'd have loved to have seen skinny dipping, scooted away like she'd been given an invisible hundred dollar tip.

Spanster shrugged. "*Some*," he said, and he handed me the bottle. Alanda had already opened it. "You here on vacation?"

I shook my head. "Business trip," I said. "Business has been...uh...a bit weirder than expected."

He laughed. I heard "fee fi foe fum" in my head because he could have done that voice bit easily.

"Welcome to the Big Island," he said. "The volcanoes generate distortions in the magnetic field of the planet. Anything can happen here. Takes a particular type to stay more than a couple of days."

"What type is that?"

He settled back, sucked in a huge breath and I could tell he was about to orate. I sniffed the hooch, decided I needed it badly and—bypassing the glasses Alanda had brought with the bottle—chugged it straight up.

"You see, my friend," he said. I was pretty sure he could have cared less about hearing my name by that point...an audience was all he needed, even if it was just one slightly drunk and more than slightly freaked guy. "You have to be willing to accept wider truths. Bigger realities. The reality is that Truth (sounded like it was being capitalized) is a pretty elusive little wiggle-worm, and it doesn't want to be caught. The chase is a big thing in our universe.

"And that is the trick. We convince ourselves that all these solid objects are what's real: these coconut palms, the concrete pool skirt, Alanda's butt—yes, I saw you staring. Only primitives would think there are things around us we can't see. But you know what? The primitives are *right*!"

He slammed his open palm down on the table beside his chair for emphasis and his drink, something with a pink umbrella and a purple plastic flamingo swizzle stick, tipped over and spilled across the wood.

"Need a refill!" Spanster hollered over at the bar.

Without missing a beat he was back on his soapbox.

"You see," he told me, "death is a material thing. Spirits—now they're somethin' else. Ever seen any of those ghost documentaries? Sure you have. Well, there's too much of that stuff for it all to be made up by a bunch of folks missing folks. EVPs, you know about those?"

I shook my head. I did know about them and I did watch some of those shows, but I wasn't about to get all chummy on the topic until I was sure he wasn't a coconut himself.

"Sure you do!" he said. "Electro voice phenomenon. They record the stuff all over the place all the time. You don't hear it, but it shows up on the recording. I'm sure a lot of it could be hoaxed but some of those shows go lots of places and investigate and they'd have to have an awful lot of people sworn to secrecy if they were faking it all. And believe me, the only folks who can swear that many people to secrecy draw paychecks for their work. They don't drive around in vans and stay up all night recording empty houses."

I nodded. "Okay," I said. "Yeah, I know what you mean."

"Right. Well, here in Volcanoland the lava—sorry, the *magma*, gotta get that right—is loaded with magnetic materials. They make the rules different." He leaned in close and spoke quietly for the first and only time. "What I'm saying is that if you see a ghost here, there's a damn good chance you did."

I just stared at him.

And he just smiled. Alanda swayed in gently, dropped off another drink, cleaned up the spilled one like a whirling dervish and hustled right back off toward the bar. I chugged more of the bottle and watched her ass without shame.

"What makes you think I might have seen a ghost?" I finally said.

"You look like you did. Am I wrong?"

"I don't know what I saw," I said. "Bats swarmed my car, drove me off the road and when they finally cleared off I thought there was a woman standing in front of the car. But I was out in the middle of nowhere and then she vanished, so ..."

I trailed off, wondering if I'd just taken bait and he was playing the line out.

"Sounds like a ghost to me," Spanster said. "Though I admit I can't explain the bats."

I hadn't even realized it was getting darker out there until the skies opened up on us in the next moment. Big drops, heavy, salty and warm, bombarded us like vertical machine gun fire. I got to my feet, expecting him to do the same, but he just sat there getting carpet bombed by tropical rain.

"Nature boy?" I said. "Or do you need help up?"

"The former, I suppose," he said. "Please feel free to seek shelter though."

That was the plan. It seemed a bit odd to leave him out there in what was already a downpour, but I was two steps toward doing that when he stopped me.

"Hey! Let me give you my card."

Good thing it was one of those fancy laminated ones. I nodded and thanked him.

"I'll be seein' ya around," he said.

Seemed unlikely, all things considered.

But the unlikely was quickly becoming the norm for me.

~

Day Two.

Spanster was gone the next morning.

Okay, make that the next afternoon. I'd finished off the bottle in my room and fallen asleep to the sports news recaps you get around four in the morning. I kind of wanted to know if he'd sat through that whole rainstorm, but not only was he nowhere to be found in the pool/bar or lobby areas, he wasn't even on the hotel register.

"Oh," the concierge said when I described him,

looking no doubt into a pair of very bloodshot eyes, "you mean the Colonel. He's not a guest. He just hangs out here. He lives out in the forest somewhere, off the grid. I hear it's really hard to find him and he's got guards. Comes here to slum and impress strangers with ghost stories."

"And sit through rainstorms."

"What? Oh yeah." The concierge smiled. "He doesn't even care if there's lightning, I've heard. Night crew say they've had to beg him to come in so they don't have to call the police."

"Wow."

"He may be back tonight. Apparently he tends to show up for a few days in a row and then disappear for a week or two."

"I'm leaving this afternoon," I said.

"If you have a card," he said, "you could leave it at the bar..."

"Oh yeah," I said. "I think he gave me a card. It's probably in the pocket of the shirt I had on last night."

I thanked him, caught a cab and spent the ride fumbling through my suitcase.

Couldn't find the card.

Figured I'd left it in the hotel. It had probably fallen out on the floor and I hadn't noticed it. By the time I came to this reasonable conclusion I'd gone through everything—thoroughly—and things had gotten scattered and strewn so badly that in the end I was obligated to stuff my undies back into the case soiled with not only my own remnants but also a stew of Satan knew how many passengers' perspirations, secretions and excretions.

I'd just gotten settled into my ambassador class seat when the captain announced safety checks. I'd cut it that close, but good enough. I was on my way home. I settled back into my seat and tried to forget about bats, ghost women and big weirdoes sitting in downpours sipping cocktails by hotel pools.

But the weirdness was not to be left behind.

The cabin was only about half full, which suited me fine: I wanted my semi-privacy, if indeed that was the best I could realistically hope for. I had an empty seat on each side. The attendants drew our shades about ten minutes after we leveled off and asked us if we wanted to see the in-flight movie.

"Do I dare hope for a work of art?" I asked the young man with the neat haircut whose manicured nails surrounded a ten dollar headset made of only the cheapest Pacific-glutting plastic.

"Our featured film this evening is A Midsummer Night's Dream about Werewolves, sir."

"Well...okay, then!"

He didn't get my sarcasm. I had to shrug off the headset.

I closed my eyes. But not for long.

"Excuse me."

I looked up at the guy, whose suit alone told me he wasn't used to having to be polite. "Yeah?"

"I was sitting up front," he said, "and it's too close to enjoy the movie."

He wanted the seat next to me. I should have moved over and put a space between the two of us but I was too comfortable. I told him to help himself.

"Thanks!" he said, sitting down. "Brad Traynor," he said, the second guy to volunteer his identity without my asking in the past day. "Appreciate it."

I felt sorry for him with his hand hanging out there so I shook it.

"Hey," I said, "nice to meet ya. Enjoy the movie."

In minutes he was grinning like an idiot and staring at the flick, which from the looks of it might not have been quite as awful as the modern hybrid title suggested. Advertising. Whatever it takes to catch the tiny attention span of the masses and tickle it with a mindworm. Last summer the big hit had been some goofy mash-up called Little Women…with Big Guns.

He kept shifting and I heard his stomach growl. About a half hour into the movie he got up fairly abruptly, cursing softly and excusing himself. He looked pretty upset at having to leave his headset behind, but it was obvious that nature was calling.

He was gone for twenty minutes.

"Rough one, huh?" I said as he sat back down.

"You have no idea," he said.

He sat back down and I noticed right away that he was wearing gloves.

"Cold hands," he told me when he saw me staring at them.

"Sucks," I said.

He put his headset back on, although it wasn't easy because of the gloves. Watching him fumble with the tiny cords, I told him he should at least take his gloves off for that task.

"Oh no," he told me. "I've got it."

He did. After about two minutes of struggling, that is, by the end of which I was about to just grab the damn thing out of his hands and straighten it out for him. But he finally got them sorted out and went back to the movie.

I watched the flick for a minute out of curiosity. This is what I got: Apparently Puck the Fairy was a magical ninja. He'd been playing it cool and holding back but now he was cutting loose on—as the title suggested—werewolves.

I tried to shut out both annoyances, both the fidgety exec with the cold hands and the anything-to-get-a-reaction movie.

I must have fallen asleep because the lights were back on the next thing I knew. The movie was over and food was being served. I looked over at Traynor and saw him slumbering, earphones more or less pulled from his ears by his own movements.

I happened to look down at his left hand. He'd fallen asleep clutching his armrest and then slumped such that a gap had opened between his glove and the cuff of his suit jacket.

His wrist was blue.

The sight of the pale blue dye—that's what it had to be, I figured—triggered something in my memory. Didn't take long to narrow it down as I kept staring at the discolored flesh.

The Curse of Lono.

On Hunter S. Thompson's flight to Hawaii at the outset of that book, I remembered quite clearly, the Good Doctor shares the cabin with a businessman who had (as Thompson correctly guessed) not quite been able to hang onto his drug suppository all the way to his destination. Traynor had gone fishing out of desperation and ended up with a disinfectant tattoo that wouldn't be easy to remove.

I was still staring at the wrist when it began to move. I glanced up and saw the attendant gently nudging Traynor's right shoulder. I smiled up at him, happy that he'd accidentally kept Traynor from awaking to find me staring goggle-eyed at his incriminating stain.

It was funny watching old Brad eat his entire meal, or try to, anyway, with just his right hand. I ignored his obvious clumsiness and focused on the slightly chewy slab of no doubt highly radioactive Pacific fish that the airline was poisoning the whole flight with that particular evening.

"Sorry you missed part of the movie," I finally said as he spent thirty seconds unpeeling the cellophane from his chocolate chip cookie. "Bugs me when that happens."

"Yeah," Traynor said. "Very disappointing."

I sat there hiding a grin. I was pretty sure that hadn't been his greatest disappointment of the flight.

Little did I suspect I had a pretty big one coming as

well.

~

The weirdness kept piling up.

I was doing my best to write it all off as my H.S.T. fixation colliding with long shot random occurrences until the captain announced that we were being rerouted to Las Vegas.

No.

Really?

That was a little too much.

"Got a problem with Vegas?" Traynor said, hearing me mutter. He laughed. There was something about the sharpness of it, and his toothy grin, that made him come off as a shark in a suit. "Cost you a house or marriage or something?"

I told him I'd never been there before.

"Anything you want," he said, smiling like he was confiding to a frat pledge. "They got it. Believe me."

"Oh, you know the place?"

That snap of a laugh again. He told me he did and treated me to a list of celebs he'd met there. He ripped on one guy he'd argued with in a lounge because the man told him he thought a world famous female celebrity was being held in a tower there against her will and he was bound to rescue her. Traynor kept jumping back and forth between calling the guy "Prince Frickin' Charming" and "Sir Frickin' Galahad" until I was silently wishing I was sitting next to the windmill-tilting conspiracy freak instead of the judgmental corporate shit who found him so appalling. At least the other guy had a backstory. This toilet-fishing coke whore with a tie was wearing out his welcome so quickly that instead of freaking out as we touched down in Vegas I actually found myself extremely relieved.

That didn't last long.

The problem was that we were both delayed there together at the airport. For at least four hours. And by then we were buddies; you know, in the way that cellmates are buddies because they're stuck with it. He didn't mind. I had played it so close to the hip that I don't think he had a clue that I kept envisioning the roof over our heads smashing open and Rodan snatching him up in his jaws and swallowing him whole. I desperately wanted to hear that maniacal super-pteranodon's squeal or squawk or whatever.

But no, nothing coming out of the machine to save my ass from the creep.

So I took action.

"It's not all that far to where I'm going," I said. "I'm gonna rent a car and skip the flight."

Of course Traynor wanted to know where that was. I lied, naturally. I was better than a full day's drive from home, but since admitting that would have contradicted what I'd just said I found my modest knowledge of geography put on the spot to come up with a viable alternative destination.

"Roswell," I said, and I was pissed at myself the instant the word escaped my lips.

Too much of a provocative place. Why hadn't I just said Kingman? He'd have bought Kingman.

"Roswell!" Traynor said. That shark bite laugh again. "Take us to your leader, huh?"

Fuck. I had earned it.

"Yeah," I said. My laugh felt weak and probably sounded it. "Believe it or not it's possible to live there without being obsessed with little green men."

Yes, I know they are a lot less green than gray or black or blue. *Allegedly.* I love all that alien shit. I love the idea that something smarter than war-addicted psychotics might be trotting around this apparently round orb floating in a dark vacuum. Hell, I love the idea that there are guys out there trying to rescue hapless celebrity damsels in distress from skyscraper prisons in Sodom, U.S.A. More power to all that stuff.

But I had to stifle all that to try to shake this guy.

"That's a hell of a long drive," he said. "You're throwing away the rest of your plane fare to boot. They won't reimburse you."

"I don't care," I said. "The company can worry about it. I'm tired and I'm going home."

He asked me if I was sure and I said yes and held my breath. I could tell he was considering his own situation, and I was sincerely hoping his final destination was in a different prime direction.

True to my luck, it wasn't.

The ride, I should tell you now, did not play out even remotely as I'd envisioned it.

That was both good and bad.

~

Not once in my life before that trip had I picked up a hitchhiker. That late afternoon, with the sun scorching the new-smelling interior of our rental, it happened before I realized I was hitting the brakes and pulling off the road.

"What are you doing," Traynor said. "Are you nuts?"

"There are two of us," I told him as we ground to a halt a few yards ahead of the woman in the frayed jeans cutoffs and halter top. "Plus if she's got a gun or a knife I'd like to know where she's hiding it."

She jogged up to us and bent over to check us out through the passenger window. I smiled.

"Where you going?" I said as I pushed the button and rolled Traynor's window down.

"Flagstaff?"

"Going right through it."

I don't know what she thought of Traynor but she didn't seem to be too worried about me.

"Right on. I can chip in for gas."

"No problem," I said. "I'm traveling on the company's dime."

She jumped in the back and unloaded her backpack and bedroll on the seat behind me.

"So you guys business partners or something?"

I don't know if Traynor said no before I did or not. Close either way.

"Our plane ride came up short. We're going home in two dimensions."

"Nice. I'm Tiela."

I glanced in the mirror. She was attractive, but no teen as her clothes suggested. I guessed her age at around forty.

Traynor and I introduced ourselves. He kept sniffing at the air oddly and I finally realized why: Tiela reeked of used ganja. She didn't seem too worried about it though.

I guess she was picking up on us detecting her all-natural perfume though.

"You guys wanna burn one?"

I looked back over my shoulder.

"You won't take gas money," she said, "I'll pay you back this way."

I caught Traynor staring at me, not her. I met his gaze.

"What do you think?" I said. "Long trip ahead."

"Indeed," Tiela said. "Real long. This is some special stuff."

"You'll impair your driving," Traynor told me like he was scolding a kid. "Don't do it."

All I could think about was that he couldn't be a bigger dick if he were stoned. HAD to help.

"I could use a buzz," I said, and I meant it. "Long day, lot more of it left."

Outvoted two to one, Traynor looked pretty frustrated.

"Give us some of your coke," I said, and it kind of shocked me to hear myself say it since I hadn't done any in a decade. "That'll balance out the buzz. I'll drive like a ninja."

"Uh-uh dude," Tiela said, shaking her head. "Ninjas don't drive. They arrive in black helicopters."

I was starting to like her. I mean, I'd liked her better than Traynor from the first word she'd said, but that wasn't saying much.

Traynor insisted on taking his jacket off and stowing it in the trunk so that it wouldn't smell like weed and (possibly, I didn't know yet) burnt Zig-Zag paper. Back on the road, he kept his window partially rolled down to suck out secondhand smoke and did his best to stay clear of Tiela and yours truly as we passed her pipe back and forth.

Despite his efforts Traynor ended up high too.

"It's making me hungry, dammit."

He was a creep sober. He was a grumpy whiner high.

I figured maybe the coke would help so I pestered him about it.

There we were, screaming down that sweltering strip of bloodstained asphalt at nearly ninety miles an hour, our fog of weed vapor obscured from the disinterested eyes of coyotes and buzzards by the rental's tinted windows.

The problem was not the weed. It never is.

The coke made us want to drink.

~

Cocaine is a morphing entity, one of the most fiendish and diabolical and relentless whore monsters in the pitifully underachieving annals of modern society. First it assumes the aspects of a siren, a beautiful creature luring you sweetly into the thrilling embrace of its eternally cool arms. Then it becomes a phoenix, your mount on a soaring trip through the clouds, where you converse in giddy rapture with angels (or whoever you happen to be around, doesn't matter.) As the journey peaks it becomes a remora, sucking onto your shivering belly and enjoying the ride. And like a remora it's not leaving anytime soon. In fact it wants company, and it will compel you to do whatever it takes to pick up more remoras.

And each successive remora that attaches itself to your gut is just a little less of a thrill ride than the last. But by then it's too late: The remoras are too many, their will too strong, and the only way to calm them—and then only temporarily, at that—is by immersing them in various percentile alcohol-water combinations.

I'd never even bought Chivas Regal before. But the bottle at the liquor store called to me the moment I walked in.

"Wee-ooooo!" Tiela said as we piled back in the car. "Now THIS is a party!"

It was, and I had no idea how it had gotten that way.

The damnedest thing was that I wasn't remotely worried about the cops. I know, that makes no sense at all. But that early evening I think I might have been a little tired of sense.

The world was not remotely sensible. Idiots and maniacs screaming at each other through their mouths and fingers, mush-headed daytime talk show hosts reducing the minds of their drone audiences to a fine broth to be ingested, no doubt, by the network execs who put the talentless gossip queens on the air for just that insidiously vampiric purpose. Hideously rich modern pharaohs drinking the blood of celebrity captives in towers overlooking the Dark Heart of Las Vegas.

I was in a meditative zone, I suppose you might say. Road and smoke and Chivas and blow and gab and coughing and orange sunlight were blending into one increasingly distant reality.

I will do my best to account for the rest of the evening, though I do so knowing full well there will be distortions and large gaps and even quite possibly contradictions. I leave it to the reader to work out their own version based on mine.

At some point it got dark and we took a side road. I don't remember why. Probably a group need to piss, I figure, but either way we ended up out in the middle of nowhere, and it must have been an overcast night because I mainly remember how dark it was.

I heard somebody vomiting.

Traynor.

He was off in the dark somewhere on the other side of the car. I had no idea where Tiela was.

Normally my stomach turns at the sound of someone else's doing the same, but things weren't normal. I listened to it all without flinching or feeling stuff crawling up into my esophagus. There was something going on, something beyond three trashed people taking a noisy rest stop on a dusty road, and I could feel it. I didn't know what it was, but I would find out soon enough.

In retrospect there was little I could have done to avoid what happened next. Make that nothing. There's really no defense against what I would fairly soon learn was called a sonic stun gun, or SSG. In open air, over a distance of at least a hundred feet, a pulse from one of those nasties tunes your thought processes to a dead air channel and knocks you unconscious in about two seconds. You barely have time to piss yourself.

Check that. You're not really unconscious, you're more in a helpless daze. It's a bit like a long Tasering as I understand it, sapping you of your physical strength. May trigger DMT responses in your body for all I know. Probably does.

But I was not unconscious.

I remember sensations far more readily than sight or sound: hands clamping onto me, being hoisted in the air, bouncing up and down a few steps and then thudding painfully onto a hard floor that rang like the metal I'm sure it had to be. I heard more stuff hitting around me, including footfalls, but about then I realized I'd either gone blind or been blindfolded (luckily it turned out to be the latter.) My arms were plastic strap cuffed behind my back but my legs felt free.

Unbound legs or not, however, I wasn't going anywhere.

And moments later the floor was vibrating, and next thing I knew I was bouncing up and down again.

I was in a vehicle, and it was moving.

~

At some point one of my presumed abductors must have noticed that I was getting a little muscle control back and struggling against my cuffs. I felt a sharp sting in my neck and was quickly off to a hot, nightmarish dreamland.

Speaking of Dreamland - that was one of my first guesses as to my locale when I woke up.

Wherever I was, the room I was in was not your standard police jail cell. Maybe prison solitary confinement, but this was Lecter-level security: thick Plexiglas with little holes in it too high up for me to even think about reaching.

The cuffs had been clipped off (along with a little chunk of skin from one of my wrists) and the blindfold was gone, but my head was pounding and the fluorescent lighting was driving my eyeballs back in my skull. These savage fuckers had no decency, no respect for the morning after whatsoever.

"How about some fucking aspirin," I yelled out when I could finally sit up, but that just made my head ring louder. "What the hell is wrong with you bastards?"

No aspirin was forthcoming, and it hurt too much to yell for it for very long. I must have sat there for hours riding it out until, just as I was about to fall asleep again, I saw lights come on beyond that glass wall.

With the long hall fully illuminated I could see my captors for the first time. A cluster of three—two men, one woman—were strolling briskly my way with lips drawn thin and in almost perfect lockstep. Uniformed, as I was honestly expecting by then, but not in the way you'd think: Their head to toe garb featured neither shiny brass buttons and colorful decorations nor any sort of insignia. Jackets, shirts and pants all, in a lifeless nearly black ensemble that left them shy only hats and sunglasses of being stereotypes of the classic super-secret operatives of modern socio-mythology.

Were these Men (and a Woman) in Black?

They came up to my cell's transparent wall.

"Hello, Clarice," I said in a slippery voice, but nobody's grim game face cracked one iota.

They were just staring at me.

"Well," I said, my head still ringing a little with every word so I knew I wasn't able to put much force into it, "I DO realize this is the age of Security Comes First and all. Right or not. I mean for my part I think not, but I suppose no one here really cares what I think. On the other hand, pardon my getting to the point right off but I admit I'm a little curious why the fuck you people decided to abduct me and stick me in this obviously subterranean compound of yours."

Still they stared.

"What," I finally said, "do you want me to dance or something?"

I saw the woman turn to the men and say something in a low voice, but I couldn't begin to make it out.

"Seriously people," I said to her back. "I pay taxes and usually behave myself. Last night notwithstanding, you won't find a mark on my record for at least the last ten years. I mean, if this is Arizona's way of handling DUIs I have to say I think it's a little extreme."

She turned back around and addressed me by name. Not surprising she knew it, considering my wallet was gone.

"Yeah," I said. "That's me. And since I haven't stolen

your wallet I can't make as good a guess as to yours."

She ignored my indirect request, although that was really no surprise.

"Why did you charter a rental car yesterday instead of waiting for your rescheduled connecting flight at the airport?"

Okay, they had my name so no problem figuring out I'd done that. Made sense, even to my alcohol soaked, light-tortured mind. But why did they care?

I decided to be honest. There seemed to be little point in lying anyway.

"I don't know why it's any of your business," I said, gathering my ganja scented self up the best I could. "Still, the truth is that the guy who'd been sitting next to me on the flight was driving me nuts, and I was trying to get away from him. But that whole stupid idea backfired, he ends up riding WITH me...and the next thing I know, I'm in Area fucking Fifty-One in what I can only presume is a human-sized hamster cage. They're right: No good deed ..."

The men had moved up next to her, so she didn't turn as far to speak to them and I could hear her.

"Well?" she said to the blonde guy right next to her, and I saw him nod. She turned back to me. "You didn't know Bradford Traynor before?"

"Are you kidding? I'd already forgotten his name."

"That last sentence is a lie," the tall blonde said. "The rest is true."

Well, that explained Lanky's purpose. Empath? Mind reader? Why not, this was obviously some black ops dungeon...freaks expected on both sides of the two inch Plexiglas wall.

And that just left the guy with the Indian or Pakistani features and skin tone, who still hadn't said a word. I couldn't help but keep glancing at him even as the woman spoke to me.

"All right," she said. "Moving on to your other

companion. You were driving, so you were the one who decided to pick her up. Why?"

I shrugged. "She needed a ride?"

The Lady in Black for all intents and purposes looked somewhere well south of amused.

"What did she say to you?" she asked me tersely.

"We were in the car for a while," I told her. "She said lots of stuff, most of which I don't remember. What, was she some kind of fugitive or something?"

She fixated on the word most, which in retrospect I probably shouldn't have used.

"Okay, yeah," I said. "She told us her name was Tiela. Is this about the pot?"

"What else did she tell you?"

I really couldn't remember. The light and her nagging were both painfully crimping my memory.

"Maybe we should give you a few more hours to think about it," she said, and of course I really wasn't up for more cold turkey hangover and she knew it. In a few hours I'd have been reduced to surviving off layers of peeling lip skin. "We'll come back later."

"No!" I was pretty desperately miserable. "At least give me some water, dammit. That's only half what they gave condemned prisoners in the Dark Ages."

But they left.

At least they turned the lights down a little.

~

Day Three.

I'm guessing it was Day Three, anyway. I had no idea how long I'd been out, but when I woke up I did so to a throat so dry that mere breathing was making me choke. The lights had come up—that's probably what woke me up—but my eyes weren't anywhere near as sensitive anymore. And most of the headache was gone.

But I was still in a plastic-walled cell that my best

guess put smack in the belly of the black ops world. I was already effectively dead if they wanted me to be. Just another missing person in an age where they'd stopped keeping count.

The woman, her mind reader and their silent companion never did come back. Instead I was hauled out of the cell through a side door by two muscular escorts armed with blocky handguns that looked like they'd been clicked together out of shiny black Lego blocks. I figured anything that looked that ridiculous probably packed a punch I didn't want to know about, so I played nice and went along ahead of them, trusting them not to gun me down in the back for no reason because...well, I had little choice.

I didn't get much of a tour, just a long walk down a bending corridor that made a gradual ninety degree turn over maybe a hundred fifty feet and was broken up by the fronts of half a dozen more plastic-walled cells like mine. They were all empty.

We came to an elevator, which I stepped into right away.

Only it wasn't an elevator, and my escorts didn't follow me. They closed the door at my back and after a couple of seconds spent pounding on the mirrored door I heard the gas.

I figured that was it. Execution booth. I held my breath until my lungs grew little claws and tried to pry their way out of my chest, but in the end I had to inhale.

Spearmint. Nice.

And then I was out again.

~

Day Four.

Another guess. For all I knew it could have been days later when I woke. My environment had improved greatly, suspicious as that seemed. For one thing I was in a decent bed, lying across the bedspread with my head on the pillow, in what looked on all sides like a spacious and well decorated bedroom. No Plexiglas wall. What's more, what seemed to be natural light was coming in through a window across the room, and as much as I was eager to look out that window my first move was to bypass the glass and bucket of ice and chug the pitcher of water that I'd spotted on the nightstand.

I almost choked half of it out in my haste. Either way it was the best water I'd ever had. But it stirred up the residual alcohol and chemicals and I had to return to the bed in a hurry or collapse.

I got up again after about ten minutes of deep breathing and slow recuperation. My clothes hadn't been changed in days, and my rank condition was pretty obvious to me. An open door off to my right led to a bathroom, which I knew I needed in almost every possible way, but my priority was getting a look out that window.

A ranch?

Why not, I suppose. I could see open desert past a struggling lawn shaded by large trees. A cattle ranch, I was guessing, although I couldn't see any from the window.

The place's doors had impressively oiled hinges.

"You look like shit."

I turned and there he was: Ward Spanster, squeezing in through the doorway uninvited. Before I got a word out he was followed into the room by a weird little wizard of a man whose almost inhuman visage struck me dumb. As scrawny as Spanster was bulky, the guy's buggy eyes almost made up for his lack of actual substantiality. He was looking at me in a way I would soon realize wasn't really odd, seeing as how he almost always looked that way.

"Funny how luck works, huh?" wasn't exactly what I figured he was going to say, but there it was. "If we don't meet by the pool I don't recognize you in the background when my associate calls from the Vegas airport to tell me her flight made an unscheduled stop. And I don't see Bradford Traynor with you, so you end up getting sucked into the dark dungeon of people you don't want to know about forever without me to pull no few rather delicate strings to get you out."

"Is that right?" I said. "What the hell is Traynor's deal?"

I wasn't really ready to hear what was coming. But in all fairness I *had* asked.

"Insider gone bad. Kind of a Man in Black with a short circuit to hear tell: A disinformation agent, originally, but then he started breaking down and telling legit info to... well, for example, poor shmucks who end up next to him on plane flights. Now as I gather it they want their people to toss the occasional truth in with the crazy garbage in hopes it'll all blend and muddy the waters, so that's why he was still out there for you to crash into in the first place. Confusion is the name of the game, my friend. But if they ended up bringing you both in, that leaves me wondering if maybe they were worried that you'd gotten nothing but the truth."

Naturally I asked him who "they" were.

"The other Men in Black, of course. There *are* systems in place, all of them running truly paperless; that is to say, all orders are given and received by word of mouth only. These people learned decades ago that the printed word is their greatest threat. A copy of a verifiable order to, say, assassinate a troublemaking senator could wreak havoc on their plans. So they work around it, and they run everything with whispers. And not for the mutual good of all mankind, I'm here to tell you."

Weak and hungry as I was, as badly as I reeked, I stood there on shaking legs listening because in that moment the information I was getting was worth the pain.

On the other hand, I was together enough to realize, Ward Spanster might just have been absolutely out of his mind. Me, I'd bought the ticket. I was obliged to hear him out. And he, in my opinion, was obliged to answer a whole bunch more questions whether he'd bailed me out of the hands of black ops goons or not.

"They Live," I said. "I get it. I love that movie."

"I'm not talking about aliens," he said, looking like I'd just relieved myself on his prized African violets. "These are simply men working for men: greedy, dangerous men, the most powerful and dangerous, in fact, to have ever walked this Earth."

I was leaning toward the rich-and-connected psycho theory at this point, I confess.

He switched gears abruptly, asking me to recall my conversation with Traynor. I still had pieces of it in my head, but not much. The guy had gabbed, and something about his personality had grated on me to the point where I'd apparently tuned a lot of it out. I remembered one thing, though.

"Destine Oliva," I said. "He was making fun of someone he'd met who'd told him Destine was being held captive in downtown Vegas."

"Did Mr. Traynor say whether the man had told him why she was being held?"

You see, I *should* have caught it then. He'd said "man" as though he knew the gender of the informant already. But I wasn't exactly on my toes. I was barely on my feet.

"I don't know," I said. "I don't think so. Maybe. Geez, THEY didn't grill me *this* much."

He apologized. Sounded fairly earnest whether it was or not. About then I remembered his bug-eyed little companion for the first time since he'd come in the room because the creep finally spoke.

"What you sensed is there," he said, and even though he was looking at me I had no doubt he was saying that to Spanster. "And our window of opportunity is quickly closing."

"Opportunity for what?" I said. "I mean I don't care

how you roll, but if someone's gonna spring me out of the Government Spook Dungeon from Hell I should at least get fair notice that I owe a couple of strangers a three-way. I mean I'll do it if I gotta—that place was damn scary—but don't expect me to enjoy it." Focusing on the little man I said, "Oh, and by the way have we met?"

Spanster grinned. "I like you," he said. "You're a funny man."

"Glad I'm funny enough to bail out of wherever that was. So what do I owe you if not disgusting all-male group sex?"

The answer wasn't much prettier than imagining myself in the middle of a foul three man centipede. They wanted me to listen to the whole gig, to know all they knew, and to decide whether or not to accept their proposition based on knowing where I stood.

~

Dolon was the little man's name. He seemed like a monk or druid to me, which was probably because he just kind of stood and listened to Spanster like I was doing. Plus his clothes seemed deliberately drab, like he wanted to blend into any given background.

He didn't react much as Spanster explained the impossible to me, but I did. Destine had a huge fan following and—despite her apparent mildness and the seeming disposability of most of her dance hits—was quite the closet subversive. She had been subtly sneaking truths about the hidden elites and their agenda into her innocuous-seeming crowd pleasers, Spanster told me, and this had put her on the short list for 3A treatment: assassinate, ameliorate and/or assimilate. In her case Destine's captors had realized that assassination brought with it the risk of martyrdom producing a reaction, as well as the potential loss of great deals of future revenue from her works, so they'd gone options two and three

166

instead (as had become the custom for the most part in the 21st Century.) Spanster showed surprising hipness by calling this phenomenon of young women rising in defiance of oppression the Padme Syndrome and told me that the defaming of numerous celebrities in recent years had been the works of this mysterious gang of thugs who had placed one of the biggest young troublemakers in a fairy tale prison tower.

"She's up there in that tower," Spanster told me, "serving the same purpose enemy heads on pikes used to in the Dark Ages. The lesson is simple—'we're paying attention, and we WILL lock you up, or worse'—if indeed the reasons for it are densely complex."

That story soon fell in with others. Spanster obviously loved both spinning extreme tales of "reality" and the looks they evoked. I could tell he was relishing my furrowed brow, and just to keep him from considering an orgasm I made sure to keep my lower jaw from dropping.

According to my presumed rescuer, the system was now precariously teetering between profit and apocalypse. As long as the money kept rolling in, everything was going to keep going the way it was... which, in a lot of folks' opinions, was shitty. But those folks didn't have money, so their opinions were effectively so much static to the ones who did.

Should resistance grow too large, Spanster told me, appearing to be part of said resistance by this point, the scales would shift toward apocalypse.

"They're ready for it," he said. "Don't kid yourself. They've been tunneling around like nasty little worms since the middle of last century. They've got *cities* down there. Purified air. Purified water. Artificial sunlight. Hydroponics on an unimaginable scale."

He looked me right in the eyes.

"They're still on the surface, among us, because there's no pressure for them to go underground...yet. Things are good enough, and they're just as fond of real sunlight as we are. But they're ready to go. They're just milking the good life they can, while they can, and when we hassle them too much—when we finally can't take any more of the bullshit—they'll flip the switch and BAM! That's it. For that matter, they may not even need to do that. Always the chance it'll be done by nature before they get the chance anyway: asteroid strike, solar flare, something like that. That's the reason they got the funding to do it in the first place: mainstream scientists, military scientists telling them mankind had to be prepared to survive an extinction level event."

By this point, I'll admit, I'd almost completely lost track of the fact that none of this had anything to do with a spa professional on a working vacation. I'd remember it soon enough, but at that moment Spanster's seemingly uber-paranoid narrative had me truly fascinated.

Heroic or simply demented, the huge man commanded my attention.

"Do I dare ask who these people are?" I said.

"I ask you to consider two primary factors," he said. "First, human nature. The buddy system. It's not who you know, it's who you blow. And then apply this to the people responsible for building the underground world. Put yourself in their positions. You can't save everyone. So who do you save?"

I shrugged. "Friends and family?"

"Exactly! The friends and family may not even be aware they have a loved one with passes to the safe haven of America 2, as I call it. They'll only find out if or when it becomes necessary."

"You're telling me the average Pentagon General Zod knows about the bunker, has access to it and can get his family and friends there if all hell goes down?"

"RHIP," he said. "Rank has its privileges. Only so many seats on the Ark and so forth."

He let me digest this.

"Politicians?"

He shook his head. "Highly unlikely. They're sacrificial props. Privileged pawns. Some of the richest are in on the deal, I'm sure. But if too many of them knew about it, the odds on someone going public with it in a damaging way would increase exponentially. The unseen wealthy of the world have no problem keeping secrets, and the military brass are trained to do it from the beginning, but those in the public eye are a different matter entirely. Sometimes conscience seeps through the desire for self-preservation, and politicians are—for the most part, anyway—still just humans. Same with celebrities in general: If they're in the public eye and still have control over their own statements, they're potential risks."

Wealthy or not, Hollywood's elite were more or less out of the loop according to my mysterious benefactor.

He allowed for a few exceptions to that latter assessment.

"I'm not gonna mention names," he said, "but if you really crank out the propaganda and make enough money I'm sure they've let you in on it. You know, like if you remake a certain H.G. Wells classic such that the military helps the germs take out the aliens at the end."

Beam effects aside, I confessed that *was* by far the worst remake I'd ever seen.

"Propaganda," Spanster said. "You can tell which producers and directors are in on America 2 by their movies and shows. It's not hard."

He launched into a detailed explanation of how award shows have been used to brainwash the masses into acceptance of specific dogma. Awards, he said, were deliberate maneuvers meant to distort reality and alter perceptions.

"You MUST agree with all of us on this," he said. "That's the message. To be accepted, to be part of the huge organism that is the human race on Earth, you should accept its values and tastes...as WE dictate them to you.

"You see? This is the ultimate distortion. Whatever message they want to convey to humanity, they do it through naming certain movies 'better' than all others, and eventually they specify one that is 'best' of all for a given year. They force the paradigm. The message is whatever they want to distract and/or pacify you, the masses, with at that particular moment. The same as news headlines. It's all a distraction. They can keep a huge segment of the populace in a virtual torpor for nearly a year now with no more than a simple political race that in the end will matter not one bit to its audience."

The guy was out there, but he was pretty hard to argue with. Part of that was due to the fact that he just kept at it.

"Music? People are saying music has become programmed and soulless. And that's probably quite true of the mainstream music that has a near monopoly these days. So if there still is meaningful music out there it's being washed over by junk...more distraction, more candy for the mind of the cow on its way to slaughter."

The gloom he was bringing me stood in stark contrast to his perpetual grin and almost jocular manner. Demented seemed the right word for it, or rather it would have had his statements not all been technically coherent (albeit admittedly well off beyond the edge of normal discourse.) As it was I decided to keep riding it out, although I readily admit that I did so while subtly rating the potential values of the room's numerous sharp-cornered objects in case of emergency.

"It's not just audio and visual entertainment that's been assimilated," Spanster said. "With mass media news now functioning specifically to keep the American public's mindset attuned to a deliberately distorted reality, and a constant feed of shallow distraction, we are experiencing as a culture the effective equivalent of surgical prep. And the procedures to come, I assure you, are intended to preserve only the self-declared 'essential parts' of our society."

I sat there staring at him for a few seconds just to make sure he was waiting for my response.

"So you're saying we're fucked," I said. He didn't flinch, nod or anything else, so I acted like that was an acknowledgement. "If that's it," I said, "then as much as I appreciate the rescue from Government Goon Central and the future history lesson here, you gotta excuse me when I say I don't get why you bothered. You don't even *know* me. What possible use can I be, and what possible good can telling me all of that do either me or the world?"

I was about to find out. And that's where it all got pretty damn surreal.

~

Day Five.

"It's him."

Dolon's declaration was front and center in my mind the moment I woke up.

I'd spent the night in that room at Spanster's ranch, most of it either wide or semi-awake, but the stress of the previous few days must have finally caught up with me shortly before dawn because I did end up jolting back to reality in early daylight hours.

I checked myself over. I was intact. If anything had been fondled they'd done a very tasteful job and cleaned up after themselves, but all signs pointed to having had legitimate privacy during the couple of hours I'd actually been out.

"He has returned," the little guy had told Spanster as I sat there, dripping from the shower that night, letting him look me over (which he did, I'm happy to say, without touching.) "Our wait in Kailua-Kona has paid off."

"Thank the Oracle," an obviously quite pleased Spanster had replied.

The rest replayed through my head as well as I wolfed

down the ham, eggs and ranch potatoes that my host had actually delivered to me in person while he sat nearby grinning at me like he was fattening me up for something.

Apparently Dolon was some kind of bizarre little mystic. Either that or he just bluffed well. In the Twenty First Century bluffing had become as reflexive as "I didn't do it!" in the previous century. When in doubt, fake it out. In an age of deliberately muddied waters, verification had become a debatable effort.

I think, therefore I am...whatever I say I am.

I'm not saying Dolon wasn't legit, but I wasn't about to buy into a bit of it right about then. After all, I didn't really entertain psychics and their kind as much more than just light and goofy entertainment. And since Spanster appeared to be taking his advice seriously from the looks of it, I was even iffier about him once the little guy had chimed in than I had been in the first place.

"Have you felt odd lately?" Spanster asked me that morning.

I had a nice sarcastic mouth-full-of-food answer for that one.

"Yeah, every day this week."

"When did it start?"

The dead sober look on his face convinced me the truth might be best.

"That day before I met you."

"Something strange happen? Did you see something, maybe?"

"I don't remember."

Okay, that was a lie. But it bugged me that he and his l'il buddy seemed to know about it.

"What had you done that day?"

"I went to the sanctuary."

"Something happen there?"

I answered that truthfully too. "Nope."

"So your day had been entirely uneventful up until meeting me poolside?"

"Yes," I said, grinning. "And it kept on that way as well."

"Well," Spanster said, "far be it from me to call you a liar, but my friend here is quite good at these things and he insists you returned to the hotel that evening a decidedly different person."

"How'd he know how I'd left the hotel that morning? Has he been spying on me?"

"He's a spirit sensitive. I had a hunch the way you behaved at the pool that night, so when this opportunity presented itself I called upon his expertise. You and I had never spoken until that night, and I knew there was something odd about you as soon as you joined me. I saw the look in your eyes. I heard the distance in your voice. You'd experienced a transformative event, and that meant there was some chance that you were the individual I'd been waiting to meet—the one the Oracle sent me to the Big Island to find. My months of effort had finally paid off."

"Effort," I said. "Drinking by a resort hotel pool?

"It was more of a vigil than you'll know."

"And you think it paid off?"

He eyed me warily, the way the wise look over a sandwich from a mobile stand.

"I'm not sure," he said. "You sticking to your story and maintaining that nothing strange happened to you that day?"

I don't know why I admitted it. Curiosity, I suppose.

"My car was attacked by a swarm of bats."

I'd muttered it, a dull confession. Spanster's grin was hideously broad, splitting that great sunrise of a face.

"What's that," he said. "A swarm of bats, you say? Well, of course that happens all the time there."

"It does?"

"Absolutely not! That's my point. It never happens."

"How did you know it *had* happened to me, then? You've been sure of it all along."

"I'll explain," he said. "Tell me what happened first. The details."

I shrugged.

"There wasn't much to it, really," I told him. "Scared the hell out of me, of course. I was lucky enough to be pretty much alone on the road, and I managed to pull over onto the shoulder. They were sticking all over the car. I couldn't see through the windshield or windows. It was freaky."

"You knew even then it was unnatural, didn't you?" Spanster said, and he got a nod from Dolon when he glanced over at him. He looked back at me. "You realized you hadn't just gotten caught in a random swarm."

"I don't know. Maybe."

He had me, but I wasn't about to admit it. As strange as it had been scary, I had known that something about it hadn't been random. It had been about me.

"So you pulled over," Spanster said, firing up a Cuban cigar and offering me one, which I politely shook off. "And they eventually just quit hanging all over your car and flew off?"

Another shrug. "In effect," I said.

"You saw no catalyst expediting their departure?"

That had come from Dolon. He'd caught me off guard, and I was pretty sure he'd timed it deliberately such that in doing so he would provoke the rest of my account from me.

I decide to indulge him.

"Now that you mention it," I said like he'd just jogged my memory, "there had been someone there. Out in front of the car, in the headlights."

"Male or female?" Spanster said, looking eager to hear my answer.

"Female," I said.

"Clothing?"

"Native American, I think." I came out of my semi-daze. "What the hell is all this?"

Had I known the answers awaiting me, looking back on things I might have just thanked Spanster, had him call a cab and send me a bill for the rescue. Thousands wouldn't have been out of line regardless of his intentions, but I didn't have thousands.

And it wasn't money he needed.

~

"You're the ideal candidate," Spanster told me as we settled into the back of his private chopper and he sealed our conversation off from the front of it with a push button Plexiglas panel. It was just the two of us by then: Dolon had left to attend to other business in one of two limos I caught sight of out in front of the ranch house. "We've never met before and you have no background of any sort that might be considered suspicious."

"What about the fact that you pulled strings to get me out of that place?" I said. "Didn't that whole little run of bad luck, bad choices and bad drugs with the hippie lady and the boring bigmouth that landed me in Hell Adjacent down there slap a big red flag on both of us: me for getting into that mess and you for bailing me out of it?"

"I can see where you would say that."

I barely felt us lifting off into the light rain but I saw the horizon dropping outside the window.

"The truth is they trust me," he said. "I'm one of them. I have a spot underground when the time comes. If I had a family and/or friends I'd have spots for them too, but I don't. I'm a loner, always have been. And you'll be happy to know that both my home and this little ride we're in are both free and clear of surveillance of any kind. It's one of the perks for always playing along; that is, up until this very moment, where we're about to break every rule they have."

"I don't know that I'm willing to die for any specific cause," I said, "much less one I don't fully understand."

"Risk to you should be minimal. If what Dolon suggests is the case, you possess the wisdom and insight necessary to do what has to be done if we have any hope to deactivate that panic button under their collective finger."

"I don't have any insight."

"You're right, *you* don't," he said. "But YOU do."

"Thanks for clearing that up," I said.

"You won't realize what you actually know until the need is there," Spanster said. "Dolon says that's how it works. Up until that moment you simply have to trust that you've picked up a purpose along with a lei on your working vacation."

"Already had a purpose," I said. "Hot tubs don't sell themselves."

"When the top dogs finally decide to pull the plug," Spanster said grimly, "they won't sell anymore without or without your help."

A sobering if debatably insane statement, one that I couldn't really ignore.

A thought hit me.

"Yesterday," I said, "you told me that you only spotted me to come to my rescue because you happened to be checking in on an associate arriving at the same airport."

He grinned the sheepish grin of a man caught in a bald-faced lie.

"Forgive me," he said. "I just didn't think starting off with 'We've been watching you' would put us on the right foot."

Eventually Spanster got around to where we were headed and what was going to happen when we got there. Tillman Foyle, a famous-for-being-rich guy even I'd heard of, was one of the true insiders according to my host. And to hear Spanster tell it, me being a nobody making a pretty modest living selling liquid relief in a big desert town somehow qualified me try to work my way into a penthouse party with the cream of the social elite and thus have a shot at getting face time with the billionaire.

Made no sense to me at all; that is, until my weird new friend explained that I was going in as his own personal boy toy.

I squirmed and made sure Spanster saw it.

"Hell, I'm not gay either," he said. "That's not the point. Foyle is bisexual, and from the looks of you I'd say he'll find you interesting."

"I'm not gonna do him," I said.

Spanster let out another one of those big heavy cartoon laughs and told me not to sweat it.

"He wouldn't do anything so obvious. Billionaires are discreet, and they don't flaunt their natures at social gatherings – not even one as private as this one."

"I gotta say I'm liking this plan less and less. How exactly can my getting face time with Foyle stop this global scheme from playing out?"

He told me the most tightly connected were allegedly never far from an entrance to the alleged continent-spanning underground network. And Foyle was one of the easiest to pinpoint: A true urban king, he virtually never left the Atlanta-topping penthouse where the party was set to take place the next night. Spanster believed that somewhere in that 30th floor complex was a hidden private elevator, one concealed so as to be invisible except in dire emergency.

"An elevator designed to only be used once."

My task was to ingratiate myself with Foyle, earn a tour and "let my new instincts take over."

That last part was unsettling, to say the least. Why did I have new instincts, and why should I trust them even if they existed?

Spanster had been saving this part, I could tell.

"Your new instincts come from the akua – the second soul that is riding along in your body, inhabiting it along with your own."

It took me a few seconds to finally muster up, "You're saying I'm possessed?"

"Not possessed," Spanster said. "Well, yeah...I suppose...in a way."

"How come I can do what I want?"

"You claim you can do what you want, and you know how absurd this all seems, yet you still chose to come along?"

He had me at that.

No clue, really, other than curiosity overcoming common sense. He would have taken me home, had told me as much, but I was actually opting for his insanity.

Then again, was it such a bad move? After all, from the sound of it all I had to do was play patty cake with some bisexual hermit, get a look around his place—Spanster said Foyle gave little no-camera tours to favored guests during parties—and figure out where the guy's Armageddon door was located. In return, Spanster had specified a tidy six figure sum that I gotta say was hard to ignore.

I wasn't sure I'd end up as a favored guest, in fact I highly doubted it, but either way I figured I'd have a chance to dine on tasty little amalgams assembled using exotic pastes and gels made from precious parts of vanishing species. Hard to resist supreme decadence, and a billionaire's penthouse party practically demanded it.

"So what is possessing me," I said to Spanster. "Demon, devil, Jacob Marley's ghost ...?"

He reminded me it wasn't exactly possession, so I tried to pin him down as to how far off the term actually might have been. He said I should be extremely honored, because from my account of the weirdness I'd experienced returning from the sanctuary that day all signs pointed toward my "co-occupant" being none other than the Last Great Journalist.

"He died with unfinished business," Spanster said. "Too soon. But part of him did not die, as Dolon and his friends had long suspected. As surely as seemingly random chance brought you to the sanctuary, then to me, then to Traynor and his rendezvous with the villains of this piece, so your…uhh…let's call him your guest, found that his own many travels eventually led him to the sanctuary."

"What happened to him there?"

"Nothing obvious. He likely never even realized he'd left part of himself behind until…well, until that was all that remained on this mortal coil."

"You're saying Dr. Hunter S. Thompson – THE definitive modern seeker of truth – left part of himself behind at the sanctuary?"

He nodded.

"The sanctuary sits where it does for one reason," he said. "It's powerful. There's something about the place. The natives stayed away from it because it frightened them. It threatened them. Only those with nothing to lose would seek sanctuary there before the white man arrived and, in his boldness and armed with his science, declared such concerns were primitive silliness.

"Thompson knew it only as an ongoing safe place, a haven for transgressors that in effect functioned in modern Hawaii much like a foreign embassy, providing diplomatic shelter from would-be aggressors. His state of mind may or may not have been heavily influenced by alcohol and chemicals when he arrived there. The narrative in The Curse of Lono doesn't make it clear, really, but either way it is obvious from his writings that his mental state was greatly agitated when he sought asylum there in the early 1980s. And that place, that power center, that convergence of forces we still do not understand, appears to have been 'imprinted' if you will by the Good Doctor's temporary residence there. His angst, his will to survive, his deeply held and hard-earned suspicions of the motives and behavior of those around him—that all stayed behind, hovering there, resonating within the land—until you came to visit."

"Why would a famous journalist – sorry, the *spirit* of a famous journalist – wait for a guy like me?"

"You ever read anything of his?"

"Well, yeah ..." I looked him in the eye. "Lono in fact, along with Fear and Loathing in Las Vegas and A Generation of Swine. But I seriously doubt if I'm the first visitor to that place since him to have read something he wrote. He's one of the most famous journalists of all time. Even devout churchgoers know his name, if nothing else."

"I'm sure there's more to it than familiarity with his work," Spanster said. "Truth be told, I took a few trips there myself and I've read his whole catalog. I'd have been happy if he would have jumped into my head. I'd have been elated. I offered myself as bait over and over. But apparently you qualify where I and likely countless others do not. I doubt either of us will ever know why unless he chooses to share his motives with you, in which case I'd like to think you'll at least consider passing it on. No matter what, though, the fact that all these events have led us here suggests to me he made a conscious move."

The thought that anyone, especially a unique and intense genius like Hunter S. Thompson, could be cohabiting my mind, sharing my thoughts, maybe even subtly directing my actions was pretty jarring. We take having our heads to ourselves for granted; that is to say, those of us who aren't actually hearing voices in there besides our own tend to do so. And it's not like you can look around your own mind for squatters.

"You in there, Dr. Thompson?"

"Shut up and listen to the man, kid. He may look like a human balloon, but that doesn't make him wrong."

Okay, I was pretty sure that was just me making things up in my head because that's simply one of the natural perversities of human nature: envisioning that which you dread. Real or not, I didn't risk any more internal dialogue for the time being.

~

Day Six.

Considering that the events of what my best estimate placed at the previous five days had more or less completely destroyed any notion of normality, I think I was adapting well. Five days earlier I'd been a guy doing a job anyone could do if they had opposable thumbs, the ability to make a smile look genuine and the patience to wait out a leaking PVC joint until the washer settled in place. As it was, I was on my way to try my luck as James Bond, which would have made a lot more sense if I had even the slightest qualification. Fate loves a good twist, I suppose. The whole You-Know-Who thing was of course on my mind the moment I got up, and I spent my first few waking hours making sure I didn't "ask" anything in my head. Real or self-fabricated, I didn't need to be effectively talking to myself.

I still wasn't sure that I was going to go through with it. My rational mind was screaming "Don't! What the fuck is wrong with you?" but I was also hearing "Don't you want to know? Will you ever get another chance?"

And that six-figure sum was dancing around in there too.

This all sorted itself out as the day went on.

It was Thompson.

He cared. Me, I wanted to go home.

But I was no longer in charge.

I think he wanted to see the rest of it. Maybe he *had* to; or, more accurately, the horcrux or homunculus or whatever I'd picked up in the sanctuary was compelled to see it through…in one way or another. My guess is he'd figured out a lot, but he hadn't actually gotten that firsthand look behind the scenes that he needed for closure.

And I was along for the ride.

I guess the part of the late, great Doctor that allowed him to deal with global travel necessities must have been what allowed me to sleep on the Eclipse EA 500 jet. I'd been in Texas ranch country, and from what my pilot told me we were right at the plane's range limits on our jaunt over to Atlanta.

"No problem," he said as I settled in. "We've got a nice tailwind and should get there with plenty of fuel to spare."

So we were counting on the wind to carry us along enough to leave us with landing fuel.

Yet I managed to doze off even with that cheerful thought on my mind.

Kalley, my pilot, woke me up with an amplified "Hey! Up and at 'em. Belts on...we're on approach."

I strapped in none too soon. The cabin hopped like we were hitting air turbulence, but in fact the jolts were coming from the landing gear. We were touching down, and a quick look out the window told me we weren't anywhere near Atlanta International. Pine forest to both sides of the runway, which wasn't getting all that much smoother even as we braked.

A remote compound. A private runway.

At this point, I was no more surprised by this than Thompson.

"Don't sweat it, kid," he told me. "And never show fear."

A sprawling one-story log building sat off to the side of the cleared landing strip, tucked right under the huge southern pines and thus virtually invisible from above. Kalley turned the Eclipse around, wheeled it almost right up to the building's middle door and stopped.

He smiled like he knew I was in for a strange ride. Or maybe I read my thoughts into his face.

"Have fun," he said.

I asked him whether I should knock or ring the bell and

he laughed.

"Nobody sleeps around here," he told me. "Just go on up."

He wasn't wrong.

"You're a special guest," Corbett Bly said. "But don't get too comfortable because you won't be here long."

Bly was a professor type, beard and wire rim glasses over a round weathered face. If he wasn't in fact running the place, he was at least one of its larger wigs judging by the behavior of the folks in the generally dirtier clothes around him. He took me hastily through the cabin and out back, where I saw three Jeeps and two Hummers sitting in a row under the trees. I wasn't sure of it—bad angle— but I thought I saw a machine gun muzzle sticking half a foot out of the back of the far Hummer.

Bad juju.

"I get my pick?"

"Yeah," Bly said, "whichever one you want. Take your pick and I'll have one of the crew drive you out to the road in it so you can pick up the rental we've got you."

The woman who drove me through the rough up-and-down woodland terrain for what felt like at least half a mile wasn't the chatty type. I don't know if Bailey was her first or last name, it's just what Bly called her. She seemed to be very focused on the task, determined to get her fare to his destination as quickly as possible, so I gave up on idle chat after getting a few distracted "yeahs" and "nopes" in response to questions both pointed and casual.

We broke out through the underbrush edging an unlined asphalt road and there sat my rental: a cherry red Sixties Volkswagen Beetle. Bailey brought the Jeep bucking up onto the shoulder and, whether she meant to or not, tested my nerve with a sliding stop that left our front end a yard at most from the back of the Bug.

I thanked her anyway as I climbed out and got another detached "Yeah" in response, so I figured I'd try my luck with the unsmiling blonde kid with the yuppie haircut who'd emerged from the VW.

"So much for low profile," I said as I walked up to him, looking over the gleaming paint job.

"Mr. Foyle is a car aficionado," the kid said, handing me the keys. "It's part of your ticket in the door."

"I see," I said, speaking to his back because he was already hustling off toward Bailey's Jeep. "What's the rest of my ticket?"

He paused at the passenger door I'd left open for him and turned my way.

"Hoping Mr. Spanster has stamped it for you."

He'd barely got in the door when Bailey slammed the Jeep into reverse, back-spun and was off the way she'd brought me, crunching through the shrubs into the woods.

I was in the car before it dawned on me that I didn't know where I was going.

This was no ordinary VW Beetle, however: For instance, the dashboard was decidedly not half a century old.

For one thing, it talked.

"Foyle's party begins at seven," it said in Spanster's voice. "Arrive no earlier than seven fifteen. You are expected as my surrogate. The monitor maps will guide you. Park in the basement garage and go past the public elevators to the unmarked door beyond them. Enter through that door."

"Thanks dick," I muttered. "Then what?"

"You'll deal with that when you get there."

Apparently it wasn't a recording.

"Can you see me?"

"If I need to."

He told me this was going to be our only chance to talk before I went inside.

"Once you're in the garage," he said, "they'll pick up any signal you're sending or receiving. Foyle isn't stupid, and he's got the best in tech like the rest of their scummy lot. Scary stuff."

184

"Right," I said, "so the only things I'm bringing to the party are my eyes and ears?"

"Well...not quite."

He told me to check the glove compartment. Wint O Green Life Savers.

"There's a camera hidden within the holes in the candy," Spanster said. "Unwrap the end when you're ready to use it. It's triggered by light and will run for thirty minutes continuously."

"You're kidding," I said.

He wasn't, of course.

He was less than impressed when I asked him how many cereal box tops the gadget had cost him. "I hope you don't come off this glib tonight," he said. "Foyle will be on the lookout for put-ons."

~

Foyle still hadn't arrived when I got to the penthouse party. Everything had worked like Spanster said it would, right down to the suspiciously-named Chet letting me into the basement garage after doing little more than looking over my ride. Every other vehicle in that basement was something shiny and unique too, with the tastes running toward Opel GTs, Panteras and the like.

I found that nondescript door past the public elevators and to my relief there wasn't anyone on the other side of it: just another elevator that looked like a broom closet until you went in, turned around and saw the control panel buttons between a pair of grimy mop handles.

Was that all it took to fool the public? If I hadn't gone in, realized there was no place farther to go and turned around I wouldn't have even given it a second thought. Janitor closet for the garage.

I pushed the button on top because it had an upright triangle on its face and the next thing I knew I was hurtling upward so fast my knees buckled. And the noise

—well, there wasn't any.

I missed that silence the instant the door opened and I found myself facing a glittering, glass-tinkling throng of parasitical 21st century socialites, clad and half-clad and basically unclad in elegant vestments fully befitting the world-devouring capitalism that had them atop Tillman Foyle's tower waiting for their lord to appear.

Luckily I got nothing more than a few quick glances before the slithering crowd wrapped back up in itself again. I stepped out of the elevator and right off the bat realized that no one there was staring into a cell phone. Not one of the dozens around me, anyway.

It was all about the chatter. Strangulated jazz muzak had already conceded to the rising and falling waves of gab as I trod gingerly into the midst of it all. The party was for all intents and purposes a single throbbing organism, alive with internal communication like some deviate elitist sea anemone, some nightmarish jellyfish of the artificially perfect upper crust.

I headed to the bar for sweet relief to steady my nerves. I don't remember making eye contact with the bartender when I gave my order, but I sure did so when he set the bottle of Wild Turkey and a glass down. For one thing, it wasn't what I'd ordered.

The bartender smiled at me.

"On the house," he said. "Take it or I'll get you what you ordered."

I told him I figured everything at a hootenanny like that should be gratis.

His smile became a little grin. "If you don't want it …"

"Leave it."

"Shoot some, kid. It'll level you out."

That wasn't the bartender, it was the voice of none other than the late great Doctor speaking inside my head again. Once the bartender was out of earshot I replied to that voice in a low mutter.

"You're not Dr. Hunter S. Thompson," I said to the

spotless mahogany bar. "I've had a weird week and I'm detaching from reality."

"That's your call," the voice said. "I suggest you buckle in and ride it out. You need to know this every bit as much as I do. Shit, that's why I wrote: to wake up sleeping drones like you. Whatever's going on here, just play along. That's how I did it, and since you read at least pieces of my work you know that's how I ended up telling some ugly truths."

I felt like pushing it. I had to know if this was legit.

"Didn't you end up writing sports columns?"

"You think I didn't have a reason?"

"Did they...did they kill you?"

"Really doesn't matter either way. The ugly truth is they'll kill anyone. Their own blood, their best friends. Each other. Sharks get a bad rap: True they'll gut one of their own and eat him alive if they smell his blood, but they're not the ones that inflict the original wound. And of course they'll kill *you* the instant you're worthy of concern. Which would make my risking what's left of me on this mortal coil a pretty big fuckup if we don't pull this off and get out with your skin. And believe me, after watching those idiots score for decades I have no intention of letting you screw us both. Now drink up, sonny, and let's see if we can't use all our well-learned politesse to save our miserable souls from waste."

I opened the bottle.

I couldn't remember whiskey being that unobjectionable before.

Before I knew it I was a third of a way through the bottle—and deep into an internal dialogue that I'm sure the reader likely believes, as did I at the time, to be simple wishful thinking. I *needed* Thompson's steady hand, his world-wizened edge, his bitter, hard fought rage against a self-constructed social machine designed to sacrifice its great and trusty body to sate the unbridled gluttony of its tiny, constricted head.

Foyle made an entrance worthy of the Greek gods, who for all I knew were in fact his target audience. The stealth missile elevator wasn't for him, of course, and I had no idea why I'd even been watching it when the dazzling flying saucer burst to rainbow life a couple hundred feet directly overhead. I could hear champagne glasses crashing here and there over the crowd's collective gasp. The saucer's painfully bright lights were raining down on the penthouse, making the glitterati even glitteratier.

The saucer descended slowly. I saw a couple jogging for the elevator.

"Fear not, people of Earth," boomed a great voice from the saucer, full of menace—until it concluded, "it is merely I, your humble servant."

The saucer lights mercifully dimmed and a shiny metal sphincter opened in the middle of its underside. I nearly laughed out loud because as Tillman Foyle descended through that opening all I could think of was how much it looked like his showy saucer was taking a slow, human-sized dump on us all.

I'd seen a YouTube video of a guy on some sort of hovering disc a while back, so that part of Foyle's arrival —him descending atop one, waving to the crowd— wasn't really a paradigm-shifter. But that saucer looked to be, at least until Foyle finally alit and called to the crew of his blimp on what appeared to be a wrist radio, telling them to turn on the flying lights of the black-hulled craft and reveal it as the support for the gaudy hovering disc.

He made an impromptu little speech that I only heard pieces of through the broad ring that formed around his landing spot: stuff about being happy to be there, thanking everyone, telling them to enjoy and help themselves to anything "except the furniture."

For the next hour or two—equal odds on either extreme since the Turkey had taken over timekeeping—I watched the King of the Freaky Elite hobnob here and there around the party, doing more smiling and listening than anything else…and notably not drinking anything. He was probably the only one there without something liquid in tow.

Meanwhile Wild Turkey was becoming my favorite drink. I felt like I was handling it pretty well as the bottom of the bottle drew near. I felt like my wits were being sharpened, not dulled, and I waited like an octopus under a rock for my chance to…what was I supposed to do?

"Ingratiate yourself. Impress him. Get him to take you on a tour of the place and look for that escape route."

Oh yeah. Thanks Doc.

Sounded like a longshot.

Thompson's spirit wasn't done with me yet.

"Do you want to settle for being a mindless little drone *all* your life? You have a chance to peek behind the door, see what's really going on. Get *evidence*. This brain dead society wants evidence, and from what I've seen riding around in your head lately even THAT may not be enough. But if you don't try, well, then you're part of the problem."

I was only gonna take so many insults, particularly from inside.

"Why do you care?" I said to In My Head HST. "You're a fucking horcrux."

"What?"

"Surely you know Harry Potter."

"Of course. Martians know it. But a horcrux is something you make on purpose."

"Great," I said in my head. "Then you're just a fluke."

"Maybe that's the only hope your dirty world has," the voice said calmly, "a fluke."

While I was distracted with my inner dialogue I missed a shot. Foyle was passing by, wrapped in only three admirers.

And that, interestingly enough, was the last I saw of

him at the party. I guess he was giving the trio that tour I was supposed to be in on, because as I watched the four of them they headed into the penthouse apartment itself. I could see them moving as shadows behind the polarized floor-to-ceiling glass panels surrounding his foyer and then they were gone.

Shit.

I drained the bottle, left a ten on the bar and wandered off. There was no one anywhere near that door they'd gone through, and hardly anyone seemed to be paying attention to that area. So I quietly sidled over there, taking my time, staring up at the warning lights around the black blimp like I was really about that. Eventually I found myself right next to the doorknob, and of course that was pretty much impossible to resist.

It clicked and turned. I glanced around. Nobody was looking my way.

"Do it, kid. Buy the ticket ..."

I remembered the line well.

"...take the ride," I muttered, and pulled the door open just wide enough to slip in.

The foyer was dead still. *Too* still. I couldn't even hear Foyle and his guests, though I could see a lighted hallway ahead up half a flight of broad slate stairs. I should have been drunk, and maybe I was, but if so I can't account for how well balanced I was as I removed one shoe at a time and glided across the floor in my fancy new black silk socks.

I sprinted up the stairs like Sir Charles Phantom the Notorious Litton from Pink Panther, my feet barely touching each one, and zipped across the landing to get a peek into the crosswise corridor beyond.

The hall was empty, but I could hear something. Distant voices.

I cupped one ear and then the other to figure out if they were coming from left or right, but it was hardly an exact scientific method so I ended up guessing. I had my wits about me enough to realize I should search the quiet end of things first.

The great thing was that if there were cameras inside the place they weren't conspicuous. The only decorations in the hallway were modern reproductions of late eighteenth century light sconces staggered down both walls, their trios of forty watt candle flame-shaped bulbs creating a pleasantly moderate amount of yellowish light. The carpet was also relicky, a more tastefully colored and patterned version of the thick hallway carpeting from Kubrick's version of The Shining. The thick aspect made me even quieter as I tiptoed down the hall to the right, casting occasional glances back the other way to reassure myself of my continued solitude.

"The wealthy tend to be savage bastards one way or another, kid," Thompson told me as I neared the left turn at the end of the hall. "You're doing great but watch out for traps."

"How do I do *that*?" I asked the voice in my head.

"I wasn't a second story man, so I don't know."

"Thanks."

"Hey, we're both feeling our way through this."

"Yeah, but I'm the one with a physical ass on the line."

"If they catch you, just say you were looking for the bathroom. And act drunk because you've already been to the bathrooms on the terrace."

Act? My whole world was weird and dizzying, so no problem.

I reached the corner and peeked around.

Where was everybody? Why wasn't I being summarily kicked out?

There were two doors around that corner, one about halfway down the hall on the left and the other at the hall's end about thirty feet away. I found myself heading down that way and was at that first door before I even realized it. I stopped and listened.

Nothing.

I was just about to move on when I thought I heard something. So I listened a little more, putting my ear right up against the door.

I had no idea what I was hearing: electronic hums and clicks, a soft bubbling sound that came and went...I was picturing a room-sized fish tank until I heard the jabber. Like monkey gibberish, but lower. Just a little burst of it, and then another.

"Open the damn door, kid, and don't forget that Life Saver roll."

Oh yeah ...the roll with the tiny camera in it. I took it out of my pocket and looked it over.

"What if I open it and there's nothing to see?" I asked Hunter-in-my-head.

He didn't seem inclined to answer.

By then I felt like I'd gone beyond borrowed time and was conducting my exploits in some sort of slip-space in time, some gap I'd fallen into, some rend possibly created by the schism between the Me of a week ago and the Me of that absurd James Bond moment.

I should have been under arrest. There should have been sirens going off, red lights flashing and way too many soulless clone security officers in unmarked thug uniforms hammering me to the floor and disjointing my shoulders to make sure their plastic zip ties were tight enough around my wrists.

"You give in to paranoia and we're both doomed."

He had a point, not that I was in the mood to concede it. Somehow nobody seemed to know (care?) that I'd invaded the inner sanctum of one of the Richest Men in Godless Creation and was tiptoeing around listening through doors. Was that right?

Buy the ticket ...

I didn't do what Thompson wanted me to do. For all I knew I was losing my mind and the voice was all me enabling myself to go off the deep end.

But thoughts of Ward Spanster and his weird little guru

Dolon reminded me that I wasn't the only one who thought I'd been—well, let's just say it, possessed. Spanster had sponsored me or I wouldn't be here and Tillman Foyle would still be just another Richard Branson wannabe I was unlikely to ever see in the flesh.

As I said, I didn't try that old school doorknob that hung there tantalizing me. There was another door, and I figured that one needed a closer look before I committed to playing peekaboo with who in Red Hell knew what behind that first door.

I danced up to it, hearing Pink Panther theme music of all things in my head. This wasn't funny. If I got caught I wasn't going off down a cobblestone street in the back of a paddy wagon with its siren going da-DEE-DAH-DEE da-DEE-DAH-DEE. With this kind of money around me I would simply vanish, and no one would know my final disposition. Least of all me.

I couldn't hear anything through that door. Like everything else in there to that point, there was no hint of actual security devices in or around it: just a heavy piece of beautifully carved ghost tree from the former Rain Forests of either South America or Indonesia, its almost black wood polished to perfection and fitted with a tasteful pewter-finished handle. No key card readers or retina scanners or fingerprint matchers or anything remotely tech.

Looked like I could just turn that lever and step right in, same as with the other one.

Is there such a thing as too much freedom? Too much leeway?

For sure there's such a thing as self-delusion.

"Turn the damn handle. Quit stalling."

"I thought you wanted me to check out the previous one?"

"This one's quieter. Of course, there may be a silent alarm on it that you'll trigger when you open it, but that's true of both doors."

"Well, how will I know if *that* is the case?"

"You probably won't."

Thanks Doc.

That bottle was still keeping my mind in the ether, floating—yet I managed to focus enough on the issue to realize that the horcrux spirit of Thompson that was cohabiting my body really didn't need to say much more. I had gone there to sneak around and try to find some kind of magic exit to an alleged network of underground cities, and I was doing the sneaking already, so ...

Buy the ticket.

Fuck it. I grabbed that lever.

I turned it.

~

I don't know why I was expecting lights to flash or a mall No Exit alarm bell to ring, but I was and so was extremely relieved when neither happened. My ice cold hand had the lever pressed down all the way but I was keeping the door frozen in place.

So far so good.

Yeah, right.

I pushed the door just a little. Still no alarms. I moved its edge completely clear of the jamb. There was a little yellow light coming through the gap, about as much as a night light might put out from what I could tell. And not a noise.

"You think they know I opened that door?" I asked the ghost of the Last Journalist.

"You haven't opened it yet."

I took that as a challenge, knowing even as I did that I was letting the Doc dictate my actions. Well, in all fairness, which one of us had painstakingly studied the Hidden Framework of world society for five decades plus?

I pushed the door open slowly, maintaining my death

grip on the handle.

A bedroom. Big, elegant, the light I'd seen provided by a stained glass lamp on a nightstand by the throwback four poster canopy bed.

I started to back out.

"What in Satan's blue thunder are you doing?" Thompson exclaimed in my head. "Jackpot, kid. Where would you keep your getaway car?"

"I'm thinking not in my bedroom."

"No, you keep it as close as possible. Especially when you sleep, and even Foyle's gotta sleep."

What the fuck. I was already breaking and entering. So I finished the entering part, quietly closed the door and took a slow stroll around the room while struggling to get my far-from-Zen breathing under control.

The guy liked his Old World stuff from the look of it. Hand paintings of stormy seas. Lots of those in heavy wooden frames on dark walls. Gloomy, really. And while the far and near right walls looked like they were made of the same glass panels that lined the rest of the penthouse proper, they weren't just polarized—they were pitch black.

Even on top of the mountain, privacy is privacy. The terrace completely ringed the penthouse, so I knew that somewhere beyond those impressively soundproof floor-to-ceiling black glass panes elite snobs lolled, doing their best to impress each other and wallow in their privilege while drowning thoughts of decay in sweet, sour, bitter and salty alcohol.

The walls of windows made my search a lot simpler, I realized. I had two other walls and a floor to check, along with sliding panels I figured covered a walk-in closet and what looked to be a large master bathroom off to the left.

My bet was on the closet doors. I made my way over to them. Sliding wood panels, old school all the way. Finger sockets for handles.

Taking a deep breath, I drew back the door on the left.

Nice suits.

Of course. What else would have been there? I almost parted them in the middle, but my instincts took over and I decided to drop to my knees and go under them instead, as it looked like I had room to stand once back there.

I was doing just that—and realizing it was too dark back there to see anything anyway—when I heard the door open.

All I had time to do was risk thrusting an arm through the row of thousand dollar business uniforms, finding the door and pulling it quickly closed.

Straight out of a cheap detective drama, I ended up eavesdropping from the closet.

One of the two voices was definitely Foyle's. Remarkably subdued it was.

The other *had* to be a voice, I figured, although the noises I was hearing as (best guess) responses to Foyle's English weren't things my vocal chords could have made. Michael Winslow could have done it, I guess, but I was pretty sure Foyle wasn't hanging with the reigning champion of human sound expression.

Here's basically what I heard.

Foyle: "You *do* realize the risk I'm taking."

Guest: (Clicking, grunting, a sort of hiss in the middle.)

Foyle: "Of course. And it's not that I don't trust your technology."

Guest: (Maybe laughter? Sounded like it. Harsh though.)

Foyle: "We're like that. Surely you've dealt with enough of us to realize we place a lot of value on whatever—shell—we're in at the moment."

Guest: (Mostly more clicks, plenty of them in fact, and one of them really weird and resonant and sounding so much like a belched question that I nearly laughed.)

Foyle: "Of course I can."

Guest: (You're getting the picture. Nothing intelligible, and if there were emotions in there they were jumbled and I can't begin to give the gist of any particular moment.)

Foyle sounded a lot different after that—well, it sounded like a lecture, I guess.

"I understand I can't know when," he said. "Just as neither of us knows can know when I'll get my chance to deliver it until that happens." He paused for a minute but his freaky-sounding guest didn't so much as make a click. "I only have one question, and I know I've asked it before: Does it hurt?"

From the sound of it he didn't like the answer he wanted.

What happened next is the weird-turned-pro moment that defined what was to follow.

I heard squishy sounds. Crunchy sounds. Popping of bones. Disgusting, repugnant noises that for all I knew were Foyle being devoured in the jaws of his guest.

Something fell heavily on the bed.

Turned out Foyle wasn't quite being devoured.

He was fucking whatever it was from the sounds of it.

I stood there listening, the most unfortunate accidental voyeur-by-ear in modern human history. Repugnant images home invaded my mind as Thompson's curiosity amplified mine and we filled my head with thoughts of what it might be like to actually be witnessing the carnal act between man and...not man.

I'll skip the details and get to the payoff surprise, which happened after maybe fifteen minutes of what sounded like a compressed all-night coke spree to my misfortunate ears. When the bed finally stopped rattling I heard footfalls.

And that's when the closet door opened.

I froze solid. The darkness I'd regretted at first—and the fact that I'm barely five foot ten—was hiding me from Foyle.

Except it wasn't Foyle who'd opened the door. I realized this when I heard the billionaire's voice coming from across the room, maybe from the bed.

"Don't take the slate Hermes," I heard him say. "I'm wearing that tomorrow."

The closet light came on.

I didn't think I could get more rigid, but I think I did. I couldn't budge. Pigeons could have perched on me. Fortunately the suits were being thumbed through shallowly on the other side, and even when one finally slipped out and disappeared I heard no reaction, no hint that whatever was grabbing clothing had caught a glimpse of a piece of me through that gap.

The light finally, mercifully, went off. The door rolled shut on its impressively hushed track. More footfalls. Two pairs now. Not a lot of talk. No clicking or weird noses at all.

Until …

"They may not be done yet."

That wasn't Foyle's voice, by the way: It was human, it was male, but it wasn't him.

As I said, the weird was just getting warmed up.

"We can return to the festivities without them," Foyle said. "I'll just explain that they're watching a video about the making of my blimp."

"Very good. It's best not to interrupt the process."

They left.

My knees buckled when I heard the door close and latch, so crawling out from under the suit rack was automatic. After a couple minutes spent staring at that wrecked bed and getting my nerve back, I went over to the door and listened.

The hall was quiet, but Thompson wasn't.

"Get over to that bed and see if you can find a sample."

"Gross," I said. "Why?"

"Because you might be collecting evidence of actual alien DNA, simp; or inhuman, at the very least."

Shit. He was right.

But I really, really didn't want to do that.

198

"You want to live with regrets? Big ones?"

"Shut up."

"Never did," Thompson said in my head, "never will."

We're gonna skip the details again. Crib notes version: I found a nearly empty bottle in the bathroom cabinet, pulled the sink drain and dumped the pills down the hole. Then I went in and collected some samples: some stinky, sticky, repulsive samples. Funny how they're not remotely so objectionable when they're your own.

Pocketing *that* little cocktail from Hell, I went over and took a peek out into the hall.

Quiet. Deserted.

I stopped at the other door on the way out and listened. I picked up on those giant fish tank sounds, muffled as they were, after a few seconds.

"You're on a roll," Thompson said. "Do it."

Shit.

I did.

This time there was no hesitation once the latch went down and clicked. I pushed the door open about a third of the way, and that was enough.

The images are burned into my mind for as long as it remains coherent, a duration I can by no means estimate, much less guarantee, at this point.

The guests who'd accompanied Foyle into his penthouse were all there.

I'm still not sure what was going on. I can't be certain what the nearly translucent green creatures were doing with them—to them—but it looked absolutely repugnant.

Hideous.

I suppose I was noticing a lot of detail because my mind wasn't ready to see the big picture.

The humans appeared to be sleeping. They were tilted back on what looked like gurney tables that pivoted at their centers around column bases mounted to the floor without visible bolts or seams. Angled about ten or fifteen degrees from normal, they were, I can only guess, ideally positioned for whatever the monsters (and I don't feel bad calling them that) were doing.

The things looked like giant frogs had thrown an orgy featuring squids and lime Jell-O infused with life and nobody had used protection. Each guest had what appeared to be a vaguely amphibian-shaped, pine green gelatin blob covering them from nose to crotch. Sticky-looking tentacles were stuck at their ends to the humans' various extremities, and both parasite and host (guessing at relationships) were undulating slowly together as though each pair was in fact a single writhing entity. The humming I'd heard was coming from some oddly sleek-looking equipment scattered around the room; the rest of what I'd picked up on through the door was coming from orifice-like holes on what I can only guess were the things' backs.

"Got a Life Saver, kid?"

I'm sure glad Thompson reminded me. The blobs weren't paying any more attention to me than the possibly comatose humans from the looks of it, so I thrust my hand into my pocket and found the roll.

I peeled off the foil and pointed the open end of the Life Saver roll at the alien rec room (or restaurant, wasn't sure.) The humans didn't look damaged, and were breathing regularly, but that didn't make the whole thing look all that much less like some kind of sinister exploitation.

"Maybe they volunteered," Thompson said. "The elite are twisted fuckers."

Once I'd gotten the whole freakish room in front of the lens of my camera I retreated. The place was creeping me out and I'd had enough.

"What about the secret tunnel to the Morlock cities?"

Thompson wanted to hit all the bases. I wanted the hell out of there before I ruined that immaculate hallway carpeting and left permanent evidence of my trespass.

"I think we have enough," I told him. "Mission fucking

accomplished or some equivalent bullshit. I want out of here."

I didn't just mean the penthouse itself. I was done. I felt like my legs were collections of stacked poles. And they only got weaker and wobblier when I realized I hadn't considered how to get back out through that exterior door discreetly.

I went up to that door with Thompson telling me I should finish the job and check out the other hallway. He was nagging, really, so I finally told him we have physical and video evidence and overheard enough to realize that ...

"Realize what?" the Doc said. "What do you think is going on?"

"You're the pro," I said, holding that door's handle and trying to summon what little nerve I had left to open it. "You take the first shot."

"Fair enough. I think our rich man is some sort of double agent, working with monstrous freaks of an actual nature that even I didn't want to think existed. Sounded to me like he's waiting his chance to deliver something— a bomb, maybe, although it would have to be a biggie or particularly dirty—to the side he's supposed to be part of; like he's going to be taken away from here by his creepy bone-crunching, clicking boyfriend from outer space when he gets the job done."

I digested that slowly, fidgeting with the door handle.

Realizing I was in the foyer and could see out through the polarized windows, I went over and did just that.

"Your turn," Thompson said in my head.

"As insane as all that sounds," I replied, "I have nothing better. It's what I heard too."

"Do you think that's why Spanster sent you here, maybe—what he expected you to find?"

I hadn't thought about that at all.

"I can't answer that," I finally told him. "You *know* I can't."

The door handle turned in my hand.

I jumped back. The door was opening and people were coming in.

I panicked. Yeah, the Doctor was kinda shocked too. Shame on him for expecting more.

"What the hell are you doing?" he said as I jerked the door out of the nearer guy's hand, tucked around the door without a word and hustled off toward the elevator at what was in all honesty pretty much a run. "Shit, you may as well shriek your way out at the top of your lungs too if you're gonna do that."

I didn't. I did slow down just a bit. I did not look back. I did expect to hear somebody yell something at my back.

But no one did.

I reached the elevator just as what had to be twins emerged. They looked pretty decent but if ever there were a time that wasn't the time, that was the time.

I shot past them, looking blue in the face I figured, and went for the control button with the inverted triangle at the bottom of the panel.

The door probably only took about five seconds to close, but it felt like forever as I stared back the way I'd come, marveling at the fact that not one person seemed to have noticed my quick exit from the penthouse and/or my scurry over to the only way out.

From the looks of it, no one cared. They were chatting, drinking, flirting, hitting on each other, wrangling deals, showing off, plotting corporate takeovers they likely hadn't the balls to pull off—but not one of them was paying the slightest bit of attention to me.

The elevator door closed.

J.H.C. that thing was fast. I dropped like America's 21st Century credibility, damn near in free fall from the feel of it. My heart couldn't have been pounding harder if I'd just run a fat line of coke the length of an anaconda.

And then I had weight again, and my knees were losing the battle to keep me upright.

Stopped.

The elevator door opened. I hadn't even had time to wonder if I might have company waiting for me down there, ready to haul me right back up to Foyle. And that was just as well, because there was no one there and I would've ended up piling that stress on the rest for no good reason at all.

I was halfway out of that janitor's closet with retro rockets when—for who knows what reason—that center button caught my eye. I held up and stared at it, noticing despite my feverish near-desperation that while just as round and white as the others it didn't have a symbol of any kind on it: just a white button, and no hint of apology.

Damn, that was suspicious. HST thought so too.

"You don't think …"

"No," I told his voice in my head, speaking aloud but low, "and I don't plan to either."

I jetted out of the elevator and took WAY too long to find my ride. I was out of breath and gasping soft curses when I finally got to it. I was probably delirious. If not, I should have been: In my pocket was evidence of some apparently parasitic, quite possibly sexual goings-on in Foyle's primary residence. Burned into my memory were the sounds of Foyle himself engaging in rather energetic inter-species mating featuring some kind of bone-popping, shape-shifting being of intelligence and power. So as I fought to get the authentic non-electric key into the driver's side door lock, putting a few scratches in that cherry metal finish in my barely functional state, all that mind-boggling insider info was overwhelming my rational thoughts.

Otherwise I wouldn't have sat there for at least two or three minutes before starting the car. If that Wild Turkey fifth was still working I was on top of it, because as I backed out of the space and looked for the exit signs and arrows my goal couldn't have been any clearer.

That gadgety dash scared the shit out of me.

I couldn't have been more than a car length outside the building when Spanster's voice rang out.

"You're out awfully early," he said, and I jumped, twisted the wheel and nearly ran into the back of a parked car.

"Shit, man, don't DO that!" I hollered back.

He got an insincere-sounding "Sorry" in so that he could quickly get to the point.

"Were we successful?"

"I've got...something," I told him. "What do I do with it?"

"Bring it back to the compound. The GPS map will guide you."

It did, and I arrived at that same spot where I'd picked up the VW to find good old cheery Bailey waiting with the kid who I guess had rented my ride and was off to return it under somebody else's name. I jumped into the kid's seat next to Bailey and she gunned us straight into the underbrush.

"Nice to see you again too," I told her.

"You found it, huh?"

She didn't look my way—her focus was strictly on our scary-ass joyride through the woods.

"I found *something*, anyway," I told her. "Wanna see it?"

That got her to look my way. Was that a smile? Barely if so.

"Of course," she said. "But Mr. Spanster wouldn't be pleased if I saw it first."

"Okay, but you'll have to wait a while then. And fly to Texas with me."

"You're not going to Texas. Spanster's on his way here."

~

204

Day Seven Revisited.

My sponsor arrived shortly after midnight, dropped off by Kalley on another slow loop-around of the secret landing strip. His eyes lit up when he stepped in the door and saw me.

"Well now," he said. "Have you saved the world tonight?"

"Huh?"

"He means," Thompson said in my head, "did you bring something he can use to nail Tillman Foyle and open the door to exposing whatever he's part of...aw, shit, kid, I think it's about time I handled this."

From this point on I think the Doctor was in charge, because everything I said and did seemed distant—like I was watching and listening to myself from a nice comfy chair inside my head.

"I'm gonna need cash."

That caught him off guard.

"I mean it," I heard myself saying. "Dammit Spanster, I got what you want. It's more than you can imagine. But where do I go now? Once I give it to you, what happens to me?"

I guess my sudden paranoia embarrassed him in front of his crew, because the next thing I knew we were doing a very private one-on-one session on opposite sides of a rustic desk.

"You're with us," Spanster was telling me. "You're taken care of. Now spill."

"I hear promises. I can't trade in promises."

"Look, you'll be taken care of!" He looked pissed. "I could do no less for the man carrying the spirit of Dr. Hunter S. Thompson around with him even IF he had let me down."

I was standing up. Why was I standing up?

"Okay, Ward old pal. It's been a hoot. Really. We gotta do this again soon ..."

Ummm...Doc...not to be a worry wart...but that was

sure a big, nasty looking gun he just pulled out of the top drawer ...

"Guns. *Really?*"

Fucking hell. Thompson was fearless with my body.

I figured his—my—bored tone would be that last little push Spanster needed to ventilate my forehead (that's where the gun was pointed) and search my twitching body. But to my amazement it worked. The billionaire lowered the gun.

"You're right," he said. "I'm defeating my point."

He set the gun down, not in its drawer but right in front of him on the desk blotter.

Thompson sat me back down as well.

"That's much better," Spanster said, reclining in his plush seat. "Now, what are we talking about? Did you use my camera?"

"Possibly. But I'm not sure what you're going to think of what I ended up getting on it."

I fished it out of my pocket and handed it over to his fat, clutching fingers.

He hooked it up to his cell phone. That took a while because he was fumbling like me with the Volkswagen key during my balls-out exit from Foyle's party.

"What the ..."

Figured those would be his words. Exactly. So did Thompson, apparently.

"That's the party scene you're missing out on," I said. Or Thompson said. Whatever. It hardly mattered. "I can see why you feel ostracized."

"What...*are*...those things?"

"Don't run," I said. "We are your friends!"

"Dear God!"

I couldn't see what he was watching in his palm, but I could still remember it pretty clearly.

"Good enough?"

He was nodding absently. "What about his escape route?"

"Might have found that too. Couldn't risk verifying it if you wanted to be sure I got back here with that."

"He's an...alien?"

"No, he just fucks them. And makes deals with them."

"Deals?"

Thompson told him "our" best guess as to what was going on. His jaw hung open so long I saw a fly zip through his mouth. I don't think he noticed.

"Still want to expose Foyle and tell the world about the breakaway cities underground?"

He shook his head slowly.

"What," he finally said, "and mess up a solution better than any I could have come up with myself?"

"Yeah, that does make it tough. But here's the twist: From the sound of it, something's gonna happen at some point anyway. Foyle evidently played his cards right— he's supposed to be one of the few really shrewd and savvy ones, as I said—and he's got a free ride to paradise in exchange for selling out our financial peers and whoever else is planning on riding out the whatever is going to happen underground."

"Which leaves us where?"

"Nowhere," I heard myself saying. "And that needs to be remedied."

I was truly curious as to what I had in mind …

Epilog

I gotta hand it to Ward Spanster: While enjoying a prolonged R and R in a rather pleasant corner of the Caribbean, I got a snail mail letter from him:

I am extremely pleased to report that our friend Mr. Foyle proved quite agreeable to our terms. He is a pragmatist, a trait I hold in the highest esteem. His friends in high places will likely be quite surprised when he jumps the gun. I am certain you too will watch with keen interest to see how the premature strike impacts those who...well, those who will be impacted. I suppose we will in effect be starting a war, but in doing so I firmly believe we will preclude complete annihilation. I will see you soon. Fill me a grapefruit, Doctor.

WPS

Well, that was that. IF things worked the way the Doc in My Head had schemed them, Foyle would deliver the aliens' destruction ahead of schedule. If not Rule Number One then certainly in the Top Ten is "You don't attack an enemy unless you have one." Yeah, we all know the glaring exception to that adage far too well by now: "Unless you're trying to control a populace." But in this case the populace—we "surface types"—wouldn't even know a battle was going on.

So, the "three" of us had decided, there must be two sides.

Two alien races was my guess. I mean Thompson's. Now that he and I had seen aliens (or at least some kind of intelligent monsters) firsthand, we were rolling with the punches. It all made bizarre, twisted sense: Sniveling mortal bastard collectives like the Human Race were toys for these galactic opportunists. Apparently Foyle had seen the light of that reality during Spanster's visit and had agreed to take a chance that the other side would have to show itself and thus take the heat off his premature misdeed. The unseen aliens who were sponsoring the underground city construction would get a little help and retaliate before their scheming opposition had its plans fully in place.

And hopefully, somehow, though I don't want to contemplate it in any depth for fear of seeing through the cracks, we will slip through said cracks and survive whatever goes down.

Sure, Doc, sure. Keep telling me that and maybe I'll

eventually believe it.

You're already dead. What the fuck do YOU care?

"Let's say you'd never gone to the sanctuary," he said. We hadn't talked much of late. "Some other poor schmuck would have ended up with me instead. The goddess was obliged to release me, but it didn't have to be to you. So if it's someone else who knows how this all turns out? Surely not better. Likely you're back in Cowtown picking your nose and peddling hot tubs when the apocalypse hits and you're fucked anyway."

"That's pretty gloomy."

"That's real, kid. And real is what I do. Now, let's hit the tequila bar while there are stools left."

So there it is: Me and Hunter S. Thompson, together at the end of the world. Or maybe not. Either way it's been a crazy and unforgettable ride.

And I guess it's finally gotten weird enough for me.

A NOTE FROM THE COMPILER'S DESK

Dear Dr. Hunter S. Thompson,

Truly, you Stomped the Terra, and the sage among us are grateful beyond words for the enlightenment (and entertainment) you gave us.

You've created a worldwide web attuned to your perspectives. We may not all blast Wild Turkey, drive 150 mph through the blistering Nevada desert on ether and acid and/or boldly challenge authority as few before you have even dared, but believe me when I say that I—and many others, including the amazing Misters Bruni and Hill (and cover artist Anthony C. Eldridge, whom I'm happy to know well enough to call Tony)—not only think like you, unthinking, peering behind the scenes: We love to try to write like you as well. Or paint inspired by you, in Tony's case.

So what we've attempted to do here is recall your spirit as it exists in each of our minds. Tony's artwork existed before he even had a clue that I was putting this anthology together with two equally fevered disciples. Saw it and could not avoid the wondrous synchronicity.

I knew we had something to put behind that fantastic cover when I got a read through John Bruni's tale. I read, and re-read, with something approaching awe as I realized that, fan that I am, he had mirrored your works with something absolutely new and unique in such a way that I shouldn't even have tried to do the same.

Lucky for me I didn't. Or, rather, hadn't. In order to avoid being influenced (and, as it turned out, intimidated!), though John had his story done a year ago I held off reading it while writing mine. The Doctor is In… My Head is not an attempt to become you, Dr.

Thompson, and just as well because I'm pretty sure that's what John did in the blast that is Fear and Loathing in Hell. My tale features your spirit in a flesh body, but it's a cohabitation. That worked out well for me, because I didn't have to try to match John's seamless travelogue. Hopefully, my story is at least worthy of sharing this anthology with his; this being my project, it's going in anyway.

And any great tale has a hero swoop in to save the day.

This book could have been out nearly a year ago. But the project stalled when another fan of yours, who also does impressive works that bring a smile as they recall your stylings, was forced to drop out.

In stepped Kent Hill, the Last Barbarian.

I had no idea the man was an H.S.T. fan, Doctor, but I should have. Charles Bukowski may influence him as strongly as you do, but there's no doubt of his respect and your influences in the rollicking ride that is A Savage Journey into the Heart of Nowhere. If I wore a hat, it would be off to you, Dr. Hill. Either way the shades stay on, though.

That brings us to a final salvo, a Twenty-One gun salute we'll all simply have to hear in our heads as we recall your timeless and priceless deconstruction of our society's hidden webs of control and how you boldly shone a piercing light of truth down upon our world's shadowy underbelly. Savagely brilliant.

Thank you with all our hearts, Dr. Thompson. Hope there's a little spare room in that convertible for these hitchhikers. To you we four humbly dedicate these efforts.

-- *Kevin Candela*

**UP NEXT BY
KC FROM KHP:
SINBAD AT
THE DAWN OF
TIME...
...AND MORE!**

Fire Dragon Entertainment

**... UP ...
NEXT BY KC
FROM JEA:
KRAKENSTEIN
VS.
KOALATRON!**

64362660R00128

Made in the USA
Lexington, KY
06 June 2017